Bolan had never encountered anything like this

"Do you think this is why the lockdown was imposed?" McCarter gazed at the shredded hood. "What if it's something in the air?"

Bolan touched his gloved left hand to his unprotected face. "Then I might already be infected."

"I'm probably wrong," McCarter said quickly.

"I'll go first," Bolan said. If he truly had been infected, it didn't matter. If he wasn't, then the air was okay to breathe, in which case it still didn't matter.

"What if—" McCarter said, but he couldn't continue.

"What if Brognola has become one of those things?" Bolan voiced the unthinkable. "We'll do our best to take him alive. But if he's anywhere near as strong and wild as she was, kid gloves aren't an option."

"That's cold," McCarter said.

"Better cold than dead."

MACK BOLAN ®
The Executioner

The Executioner

Don Pendleton's ®

LOCKDOWN

A GOLD EAGLE BOOK FROM

W❂RLDWIDE.®

TORONTO • NEW YORK • LONDON
AMSTERDAM • PARIS • SYDNEY • HAMBURG
STOCKHOLM • ATHENS • TOKYO • MILAN
MADRID • WARSAW • BUDAPEST • AUCKLAND

First edition December 2004
ISBN 0-373-64313-6

Special thanks and acknowledgment to
David Robbins for his contribution to this work.

LOCKDOWN

Printed in U.S.A.

Let him who desires peace prepare for war.

—Vegetius
Fourth century Roman

A warrior is like a knife. He must constantly
hone his skills if he is to stay sharp and focused.
Being prepared is more than a motto. It should
be a way of life.

—Mack Bolan

THE
MACK BOLAN®
LEGEND

Nothing less than a war could have fashioned the destiny of the man called Mack Bolan. Bolan earned the Executioner title in the jungle hell of Vietnam.

But this soldier also wore another name—Sergeant Mercy. He was so tagged because of the compassion he showed to wounded comrades-in-arms and Vietnamese civilians.

Mack Bolan's second tour of duty ended prematurely when he was given emergency leave to return home and bury his family, victims of the Mob. Then he declared a one-man war against the Mafia.

He confronted the Families head-on from coast to coast, and soon a hope of victory began to appear. But Bolan had broken society's every rule. That same society started gunning for this elusive warrior—to no avail.

So Bolan was offered amnesty to work within the system against terrorism. This time, as an employee of Uncle Sam, Bolan became Colonel John Phoenix. With a command center at Stony Man Farm in Virginia, he and his new allies—Able Team and Phoenix Force—waged relentless war on a new adversary: the KGB.

But when his one true love, April Rose, died at the hands of the Soviet terror machine, Bolan severed all ties with Establishment authority.

Now, after a lengthy lone-wolf struggle and much soul-searching, the Executioner has agreed to enter an "arm's-length" alliance with his government once more, reserving the right to pursue personal missions in his Everlasting War.

Blue Ridge Mountains, Virginia

Dark clouds roiled and churned on the horizon. Hal Brognola gazed out the window of his limousine and saw the treetops bent by violent gusts. A few raindrops pattered against the glass, harbingers of more to come. The forecast called for severe thunderstorms.

Not that Brognola was all that interested in the weather. He shifted his attention to the road ahead. It wound like an asphalt serpent to the crown of a mountain straddled by a perimeter fence. Inside that fence reared half a dozen stucco buildings. The Spider Mountain Research Facility, as it was called.

The dashboard phone beeped and the limo's driver snatched it up. "Higgins here." He stiffened, then bleated, "Mr. Harkin! Yes, sir, we're right on schedule! You should be able to see us if you look out your window." He paused. "Very well, sir. Whatever you wish. You have only to say the word."

Brognola suppressed a chuckle. The man had groveling down to a fine art. Shifting, he glanced out the rear at the four limos following his. The whole affair was much too flashy for his taste, but then this was supposed to be a red carpet VIP tour and their host was pulling out all the stops.

Higgins hung up. "Good news, Mr. Brognola. Mr. Harkin will be on hand to greet you and the rest personally."

The driver's tone made it sound as if God Almighty had

deigned to descend from His throne. Brognola frowned. He
never had been a big fan of Luther Harkin's, but he would be
the first to admit Harkin Industries was a crucial cog in America's research and development program. Some of the latest
and best inventions had been spawned in Harkin labs.

Brognola's cell phone trilled and he unhooked it from his
belt. "Speak to me," he said without preliminaries.

"The roosters have all returned to the roost," Barbara Price,
mission controller at Stony Man Farm, announced. She was
referring to Phoenix Force and Able Team, special ops units
answerable only to the President. And to Brognola, who
served as their White House liaison. Both had returned from
separate missions.

"What about the cock of the walk?" In his mind's eye
Brognola envisioned Mack Bolan—that rugged face, chiseled
by a thousand battles, and those piercing blue eyes that looked
right through you. In the perilous world of black ops, Bolan
was the best there was, bar none.

"He's due in any time now," Price reported. "His flight out
of New Orleans was delayed."

"Handle the debriefing. Have everyone stand down until I
get there. They've earned some R and R." Which was an un-
derstatement, Brognola reflected. The elite commandos under
his charge risked their lives daily in defense of Lady Liberty.
America, and the entire free world, owed them a debt that
could never be repaid. They were the first line of defense
against the spread of evil, unsung heroes who would likely
go to their graves unknown and unrewarded.

"When can we expect you?" Price inquired.

Brognola checked his watch. "It's a little past four. The tour
won't take more than a couple of hours. Add travel time, and
I should be there by seven." He paused. "I'm not to be dis-
turbed unless it's of vital importance."

"Does David McCarter throwing a fit that the fridge in the
rec room is out of Coca-Cola qualify?"

A grin tugged at the big Fed's mouth. David McCarter was the head of Phoenix Force, a temperamental Briton whose idea of health food was a can of soda pop and a candy bar. Hell on wheels, McCarter had a flair for getting out of tight spots, and for giving his superiors an occasional headache. "Have the fridge restocked before that happens."

"Will do." The big Fed could hear the smile in her voice. Brognola said goodbye and clicked off.

A gate appeared, manned by Harkin security personnel in their trademark brown uniforms. Although he wasn't fond of Luther Harkin, Brognola had to admit that Harkin Industries only hired the cream of the crop. The guards were a case in point. Brognola's ID was checked, then confirmed by a quick call to the command center. A large sign to the left of the gate announced trespassers would be prosecuted to the fullest extent of the law.

Parking spaces in front of the main building had been left vacant. As the limo bearing Brognola slid into the first slot, a knot of suits and skirts burst through the double doors. Harkin's entourage. Rumor had it he never went anywhere without them.

Higgins slid out and briskly opened the rear door. "I trust you enjoyed your ride, sir."

Unfolding from the vehicle, Brognola stretched to relieve a kink in his back. The clouds to the west were darker, the wind on his cheeks laced with more than a hint of moisture.

A hand dominated by a ring with a ruby the size of an acorn was thrust at him. "We meet again, Mr. Brognola. It's been, what, eight months since that brunch at the Pentagon?" Luther Harkin pumped Brognola's arm with vigor. "I'm glad you could make it."

Brognola wasn't. He could think of a hundred things he would rather do than endure Harkin's oily charm. But part of his job as director of the Justice Department's Sensitive Operations Group was to keep abreast of the latest inroads in the field. That meant visiting sites like this from time to time.

"Who else will be here?"

"You'll see shortly." Harkin moved to greet the rest.

Brognola had been picked up outside the Justice Department Building and whisked to a rendezvous point where his limo was joined by the others. A show of Harkin's wealth and clout, designed to impress, more than anything else. But Brognola didn't impress easily.

Luther Harkin formed Harkin Industries fresh out of college. His family had money, and Harkin had used it to hire the best scientists his wealth could entice. Harkin Industries soon became a leader in military applications, everything from stronger metal for tanks to energy capsules that gave weary soldiers a boost in the field. The Spider Mountain facility was just one of seven biotech firms Harkin owned, along with a dozen subsidiaries.

From the second limo emerged a man Brognola recognized. Bryce Chandler was a lynchpin of the National Security Agency, a lifelong civil servant who had survived the ritual cleansing by new administrations and become invaluable in the process. It was said he knew more dark and dirty secrets than anyone in Washington. It was also said those secrets were secure because he was as tight-lipped as a steel drum and as honorable as Abe Lincoln.

Brognola waited for Luther Harkin to finish pumping Chandler's hand, then offered his own. "Bryce. This is a treat. It's been much too long." There had been a time when the two of them met for lunch monthly to swap war stories. But that had been years ago.

Chandler had more white hair than a polar bear and a smile that could light up a Christmas tree. "Hal! As I live and breathe! Maybe this won't be as boring as I feared." They clapped each other on the shoulder, and Chandler suddenly pulled Brognola to one side and lowered his voice. "Just between you, me and the doorpost, listening to Harkin spout off isn't my idea of entertainment. What say we go grab us a bite to eat after this is over and catch up?"

"I might be able to spare the time," Brognola said. "Any idea why the President insisted this soiree would be worth our while?"

Chandler lowered his voice even more. "Harkin has something special up his sleeve. A major breakthrough, if what he told the President is to be believed. We're here to confirm it for ourselves, then advise the President accordingly."

Despite himself, Brognola's interest was piqued. Although he considered Harkin an arrogant jackass, the man took the research end of his enterprises seriously, as his track record proved. "Just as long as it's not a new inflatable doll for lonely GIs."

Laughing heartily, Chandler declared, "In the old days you always were good for a grin. It's nice to know some things never change."

But they did. Brognola's carefree days were long gone. Many who knew him would be shocked to learn that at one time he had been known to crack a joke on occasion. Age, and the wicked ways of the world, had taken a toll.

The other limousines disgorged their occupants. One was a small man with a pencil-thin mustache. He ran a finger across his upper lip, then smoothed his tie and both sleeves.

The other was a young woman wearing a suit. She carried a briefcase and thrust her hand at Harkin with confident poise.

"I don't know those two," Brognola said to Chandler.

"The gentleman is Gregory Merton, National Intelligence Council. I'd imagine he's here because part of the NIC's mission is to keep the director abreast of the latest research." Chandler's bushy eyebrows puckered. "The lovely young lady, unless I'm mistaken, is on the management staff of the CIA. Her name eludes me at the moment, however."

Brognola was going to introduce himself, but Luther Harkin picked that moment to usher them toward the complex. Harkin's entourage formed a phalanx, effectively isolating the VIP group from Spider Mountain's other employees. Was it deliberate? Brognola wondered. He glanced to the west a final time.

A thunderhead was sweeping across the sky and would soon be directly overhead. More rain began to fall, and in the distance a jagged bolt of lightning sheared the firmament.

The interior of the research facility belied the stucco facade. Brass, plastic and tile were in abundance, along with the occasional artificial plant. Security personnel, armed to the gills, were everywhere—flanking the entrance, along the walls, stationed on the landings above.

"Expecting World War III to break out, are we?" Bryce Chandler inquired dryly.

Luther Harkin wasn't amused. "I'm more concerned about industrial espionage. My competitors would pay dearly for our secrets. So would our country's many enemies, I might add."

The young woman cleared her throat. "Surely you don't post this many guards all the time?"

"No, Ms. Reese, of course not," Harkin conceded. "This is a special occasion. In addition to yourselves, top military brass are waiting below for the demonstration to begin. Heightened security is essential."

"Is that why you sent limos to collect each of us individually when we could have ridden together?" the woman responded.

Brognola liked her. She had a no-nonsense air that was refreshing. As the entourage steered them toward a bank of elevators, he introduced himself.

"Lucille Reese." Her handshake was firm. "A pleasure to make your acquaintance." She studied him while trying not to be obvious. "You must have a fair amount of clout to be invited to one of these presentations," she said.

Brognola smiled. She was tactfully fishing for information. He derailed her attempt by saying, "I take it you're not a big fan of his?"

"Harkin?" Reese snorted. "He missed his calling. He should have been a petty dictator in a Third World country.

Preferably one where they dispose of dictators by firing squad. Or, better yet, by smearing them with honey and staking them out over an anthill." She practically dripped venom.

"It's none of my business, but it sounds as if there are personal issues between the two of you."

"You're right." Reese replied. "It's none of your business."

On that chilly note they entered one of the elevators, along with Bryce Chandler and several of Harkin's personal staff.

Just then the whole building quaked and a booming blast sounded from somewhere outside. To Brognola, it felt as if a grenade had gone off a stone's throw away.

"Lightning," a staffer said. "There are near strikes all the time."

Lucille Reese shot him a withering smirk. "That's what you get for constructing this place on top of a mountain. I hope the complex has lightning rods."

The staffer held his ground. "I assure you, Ms. Reese, proper precautions have been taken. Backup systems, generators, the works. Even if we suffered a direct hit, it would barely faze us."

"Famous last words," Reese quipped.

The elevator dropped swiftly. Brognola watched the digital display. It stopped at Sublevel 12, the lowest, and the doors hissed open. More guards lined a well-lit corridor. The rest of their party spilled from the other elevators.

They were guided into a spacious chamber with wine-red carpet. Trays of food and beverages covered a long table. Two rows of chairs faced a glass partition separating the chamber from a superbly furnished laboratory. Individuals in white lab coats were bustling about.

Brognola was distracted by four men standing beside the food table. Their uniforms indicated they represented each branch of the military. All of them were officers.

Luther Harkin did the honors. "General Scott, Army Intelligence. General Winfield, Air Force Intelligence. General

Drake, Marine Corps Intelligence. And Admiral Peters, Naval Intelligence. Ladies and gentlemen, may we proceed?"

They were asked to take a seat. Brognola ended up between Bryce Chandler and Lucy Reese. Two more people had entered the lab beyond the glass partition, one a tall scientist with gray hair who began issuing instructions, the other a skinny young man who sat in an elevated chair and began stripping to the waist.

Harkin stepped to the glass and punched a button on an intercom. Snatches of conversation came over the speaker. The tall scientist was directing an assistant to prepare a syringe. "Are we about set to begin, Dr. Bellamy?" Harkin asked.

"We'll be ready when you are," the scientist assured him.

Beaming, Harkin faced his guests. "I can't thank you enough for taking time out of your busy schedules to be here today. It will be well worth it. What you are about to witness will revolutionize the military-industrial complex to a degree not seen since the invention of the Gatling gun."

Brognola saw the assistant insert the needle into the stopper on a vial and fill the syringe with a yellow fluid.

"Harkin Industries has always been on the cutting edge of research and development," Harkin continued. "This facility is a leader in developing biopharmaceuticals, but with a difference. Where other companies are out to eradicate world hunger or eliminate disease, we're exclusively devoted to strengthening Americans' might where it counts most—on the battlefield."

The assistant passed the syringe to Dr. Bellamy, who moved over to the chair and the young man who had stripped to the waist.

"Our goal is to produce the soldier of the future. To enhance natural ability to a level never before conceived." Harkin gestured. "Imagine, if you will, soldiers five times as strong as they normally are. Soldiers who never tire, who are impervious to pain. Supersoldiers, who would be next to invincible."

"Oh, please," Lucy Reese muttered.

General Drake was keenly interested. "Are you saying your people can perform such a feat?" he asked Harkin.

"Actions speak louder than words," Harkin answered. "Prepare to be amazed." He spoke into the intercom. "Do it, Doctor."

The scientist injected the yellow substance into a vein on the young man's forearm. For thirty seconds nothing happened. Then the young man threw back his head and grimaced. He gripped the arms of the chair, his veins bulging, and began to breathe loudly through his nostrils.

"Don't be alarmed," Harkin assured the observers. "This won't last long. The body stabilizes quickly." He impatiently tapped the glass. "Whenever our test subject is ready, Dr. Bellamy, proceed to phase two."

The eyes of Brognola and the other VIPs were riveted to the young man. The subject had gone momentarily rigid, then he began to flex and unflex his fingers, and he stared at them as if he'd never seen them before.

Dr. Bellamy said something Brognola didn't catch, and the young man nodded and stood.

One of the assistants bent behind a console. When she straightened, she held a long metal bar, which she handed to Bellamy. He, in turn, gave it to the subject.

"That's solid iron," Harkin stated. "From a barbell set that can be purchased at any sporting goods store. Watch what he does."

The subject gripped the bar at both ends and held it out in front of him at chest height. With an ease that had to be seen to be believed, he casually bent the bar into a horseshoe shape.

General Scott and Admiral Peters shot to their feet. "Incredible!" Scott blurted.

"You haven't seen anything yet," Harkin gloated.

That was when the lights went out.

2

Washington, D.C.

The Executioner was an hour and a half late getting into Reagan National Airport. He had to take a civilian flight because Stony Man Farm's ace air jockey, Jack Grimaldi, had been ferrying Phoenix Force home from overseas, and the backup pilots were busy with Able Team. His stomach growled as he left the terminal and made for a parking garage where the government kept cars specifically for the use of Stony Man personnel. Hefting his carry-on, he waited for a shuttle to go by, then crossed at an intersection.

Mack Bolan's St. Louis trip had been successful. There was now one less drug kingpin in the world, and a ton less cocaine. Bolan regretted, though, having to make other arrangements for transporting his personal arsenal back to Stony Man Farm. Since 9/11, commercial carriers wouldn't allow so much as a nail file on board. He wasn't comfortable traveling unarmed. He felt a shade uneasy. Almost as if he were only partially dressed.

The car was in the parking space it should be, the keys under the rear fender in a magnetic container. Bolan unlocked the door, slid in, fastened his seat belt and started the engine. The sedan purred down a series of ramps to the street. Bolan had driven only a couple of miles when his stomach growled again. Ahead, on the right, he spotted a convenience store.

The elderly Korean man behind the counter looked up

from a magazine and smiled when Bolan entered. Nearby, a mother was refereeing a dispute between her two children over a candy bar both wanted. They were the only customers in the store.

The cooler was at the back of the room. A chicken sandwich looked appetizing. Bolan was reaching for it when a tiny bell over the front door jangled and a bellow drowned out the squabbling kids.

"Hands in the air, suckers!"

Bolan dropped into a crouch. Several aisles of merchandise screened him from whoever had entered. Unnoticed, he glided to an end display.

"You heard him!" a second intruder shouted. "That means you, old man! Unless you want your brains splattered all over that cash register!"

The woman started to scream, but the sound of a sharp slap cut her cry short. One of her children whimpered in fear.

"Shut your brat up, lady, or we'll do it for you!" the first voice sounded again.

Bolan darted to the next row of merchandise and peered down the aisle. A pair of street sharks brandishing knives were responsible. One appeared to be strung out on something and kept jerking and twitching as if he had fire ants in his clothes. The other had orange hair gelled into spikes.

"All we want is your cash, dude," the druggie told the Korean. "Fork it over and we're out of here!"

The woman had her children pressed to her sides and seemed to be in near hysterics. "Do as he says, Mr. Kim, please!"

The man behind the counter didn't move.

"You heard her, Kim!" the druggie snapped, stepping closer to the old man and waving his knife. "The cash, you old fart, or I'll gut you like a fish!"

Bolan was too far away to be of any help. They would spot him the moment he moved into the open and might use the woman or her children as shields. He deemed it wiser to stay put. All Kim had to do was comply, and the pair might leave in peace. But Kim didn't see it that way. He stooped down out of sight, and when he rose up again, he was holding a pistol-grip shotgun.

"Look out, Lester!" the punk with the spikes yelled.

Kim pumped a round into the chamber and fired. In his haste he neglected to brace himself, and although he was only eight feet from his intended target, he missed. The blast blew apart a candy display next to Lester instead of blowing apart Lester himself. In the next instant, Lester howled in fury and charged.

Again Kim worked the pump, but he was badly out of practice and before he could squeeze off a second round, Lester sprang onto the counter and kicked him full in the face.

Bolan was also in motion. It didn't matter now whether the other punk saw him. He had to do what he could to spare Kim and the woman and her kids from harm. But he had to run the entire length of the store.

Lester's knife flashed in the fluorescent light. Kim cried out, let go of the shotgun and clutched at his throat. He staggered against a cigarette case, blood spurting from his severed jugular. Lester's blade flashed again, and Kim crumpled like soggy paper.

The young mother screamed.

"Shut up, bitch!" the punk with the spiked hair snapped, and came at her with his knife held low.

Backpedaling, the woman inadvertently put herself between the punk and Bolan. "Please! In God's name, don't!" she begged.

"We can't leave witnesses, you stupid cow!" The punk smirked and nicked her cheek with a teasing slash.

A shriek of mortal terror tore from the woman's throat. Her kids were glued to where they stood with fright. Death loomed, and there was nothing they could do to prevent it.

But the Executioner could. He was past the woman before

any of them realized he was there. Surprise rooted the punk with the spikes, but he recovered and lanced his blade at Bolan's chest. The soldier countered with a forearm block. Almost in the same move, he gripped the punk's wrist and arced his knee upward.

At the distinct crack of the punk's elbow, the would-be tough screamed in pain and dropped his knife. He took a step toward the door but got no farther.

Bolan's right foot flicked out and connected with a knee-cap. The punk toppled straight into a palm-heel strike to the face that pulped his lips, broke several teeth and left him unconscious on the floor.

"I'll get you, sucker!" Lester yelped. He had scooped up the shotgun. Pointing it at Bolan, he began firing like a madman. However, hopped up on drugs as he was, he couldn't hit the broad side of the convenience store.

Bolan hit the floor. He shouted for the woman to get down, but she couldn't hear him over the boom of the shotgun. Three shots thundered, each punctuated by the sickening splat of heavy lead ripping into unyielding flesh.

Bolan glanced over his shoulder and a chill seized his soul. The mother and both children were sprawled in heaps, their heads and chests chewed to ribbons.

Lester worked the pump again, but the shotgun was empty. Tossing it aside, he vaulted from the counter, the blood-caked knife in his right hand.

The soldier rose, wrath boiling in him like molten lava in a volcano. He met Lester's rush head-on, countering a flurry of stabs and slashes without giving an inch. Then his left hand shot out and his fingers clamped onto Lester's throat. A single steely squeeze and the job was done.

Flopping onto his side, Lester sputtered and gasped, a crushed windpipe his ticket to oblivion. His last earthly sound was a pathetic whine.

Bolan confirmed that the woman and her children were

dead, peered over the counter at Kim's lifeless form, then got out of the store. The last thing he needed was to be hauled into the local precinct for questioning.

No sooner did he gain the curb, than a souped-up muscle car roared toward him from out of nowhere. Lester and his buddy had a wheelman who saw what happened through the plate-glass windows and was out for revenge. His teeth shone white above the steering wheel in a vicious sneer.

Headlights trapped Bolan in their glare. He had only seconds to react. Lunging to the left, he suddenly reversed direction and threw himself into a rolling dive. He heard the crunch of tires, the squeal of brakes. Plate glass shattered in a tremendous crash, and shards rained in a downpour.

The wheelman had plowed into the front of the store. Jamming the gearshift into reverse, he stomped on the gas, causing the rear tires to spin and spew burned rubber. He was ranting, "Damn you! Damn you! Damn you!" But whether he was cursing the soldier or his car was impossible to say.

In a rush, Bolan reached the guy's open window and grabbed at a scrawny neck. But as luck would have it, the rear tires gained enough traction to send the car hurtling backward. Pulling his arms back, Bolan crouched.

The driver slammed on the brakes, spun the steering wheel, and the car hurtled forward once more. He was cackling with sadistic glee at the prospect of running Bolan down. In a span of heartbeats the car accelerated from zero to sixty miles an hour.

Bolan waited until the last possible instant, then leaped to the right. He nearly misjudged. The car brushed him, it was so close, knocking him off stride, but he was still able to spin and spring at the open window before the driver could throw the vehicle into reverse again. He landed a solid blow to the jaw that rocked the would-be killer's head, but the driver was tougher than he looked and screeched the vehicle into reverse, and to safety.

The Executioner was getting nowhere. As the vehicle lined up for another run, he cast about for a weapon. Something. Anything. His gaze fell on a fist-sized chunk of broken masonry. Scooping it up, he turned as the car streaked across the lot, its driver bent on Bolan's destruction. The wheelman cackled anew, as if the whole thing were a warped joke.

Bolan had played his share of baseball when he was younger. Little League, high school, the usual. He wasn't major league material, but he always had a good arm and an uncanny aim. Hefting the masonry, he let fly with all his might at the windshield, then vaulted out of the vehicle's path.

A yelp rent the air. Like a battering ram gone amok, the car smashed into the store, taking out half a wall. Brick and mortar came crashing down onto the roof, which crumpled under the impact. A keening screech ended in a gurgled sob, then all was still.

Warily approaching the driver's side, Bolan bent down. Brains and gore were oozing from a cavity in the wheelman's cranium, and one shoulder was crushed. As the soldier straightened, sirens wailed amid the city's stone canyons.

In moments Bolan was back in his sedan. He raced out of the parking lot and didn't slow until he was sure he wasn't being pursued. Settling back in the driver's seat, he touched a spot on his neck where a sliver of glass had drawn a drop of blood.

Bolan thought about the mother and her children. He had tried his best, but it hadn't been enough. So be it. He had no choice but to lock the memory away where it wouldn't haunt his waking hours, and forge ahead with his War Everlasting. Some might say that was cold. Some might say he was too callous. But until they had walked a mile in his combat boots, they had no business to judge.

A true warrior was more than muscle and bone, more than a walking will to kill. A true warrior also had a heart and soul, and to preserve them had to wall off the horrors or suffer the torment of the damned. It was as essential to survival as finely honed combat skills.

Bolan had learned long ago to keep his emotions in check, and it was not a lesson that came easily.

3

Luther Harkin took the loss of power in typical stride. "Please remain seated, everyone. I assure you this facility is state-of-the-art in every respect. We have redundant systems to spare. Any moment now the generators will switch on and things will be back to normal."

As if on cue, the lights came back on. But they were only half as bright as before. Hal Brognola glanced at his old colleague, Bryce Chandler, then at the young woman from the CIA management staff, Lucy Reese. "Anyone bring a deck of cards?"

Brognola's comment was overheard by Harkin. "The demonstration will proceed according to plan, Mr. Brognola. We can't permit a trifling nuisance like a thunderstorm to stand in the way of the march of Western civilization."

Harkin scanned those in the chairs as if expecting a few laughs and chuckles but received only a stony silence. He continued with his presentation. "Dr. Bellamy, be so kind as to enlighten our guests as to the nature of the substance injected into our volunteer's veins."

In the subdued light the lab workers were spectral white shapes, their faces barely visible. Dr. Bellamy held out the vial. "In layman's parlance, this is designed to enhance human performance to peak levels. A bioenhancer, in other words. Our lab designation for it is BE7722."

"What can you tell us about the chemicals used?" Gregory Merton asked.

"Not much," Harkin answered. "The formula is one of our most closely guarded secrets, for reasons that should be apparent to everyone present."

Dr. Bellamy held the vial higher. "I can say that the primary chemical component was extracted from a genetically altered South American plant. We became interested after hearing about a tribe that ate the plant's leaves to augment their strength when they go to war. Obtaining specimens cost the lives of two expedition members."

"That's more than enough background, Doctor," Harkin said curtly. He impatiently consulted his watch. "Why is it taking so long for the power to be fully restored? The utility company is under standing orders to give Spider Mountain top priority."

Lucy Reese raised her hand as if she were in a classroom. "I have a question, if you don't mind."

Harkin regarded her suspiciously. "As long as it's not about the specific chemicals."

"No, it's about this test. A syringe was used to inject that man. Yet under the CDC's biosafety guidelines outlined in their Environmental Health and Safety Operations Guide, the use of syringes is specifically prohibited."

Harkin didn't even try to hide his contempt. "The guidelines apply to biohazards, which, in this form, BE7722 plainly isn't. And the CDC merely advises to avoid using syringes wherever possible. They never issued a formal ban."

"What did you mean by 'in this form'?" Brognola inquired.

But before he could receive an answer, recessed lights in the ceiling began to flash yellow and Klaxons began bleating in shrill cadence.

"The system is going haywire!" Harkin exclaimed. "It must be due to the damn power outage."

Dr. Bellamy was much paler than he had been a few seconds ago. "No! There's a containment breach! The computer is implementing the biohazard protocols. If Code Red is put into effect, it means there is serious trouble."

"It's a short in the system, I tell you," Harkin insisted. "As soon as the power is restored everything will be fine."

Suddenly the flashing lights changed from yellow to red and the Klaxons took on a new note, shrieking like banshees.

"My God!" Dr. Bellamy rushed toward the door of the lab and wrenched on the handle. The door didn't budge. "It *is* Code Red!"

Brognola rose. He didn't like the panic in Bellamy's voice.

Some of Harkin's staff exchanged nervous looks. Harkin motioned at one, then at the door. The man hastened over, tried to open it and couldn't. Undaunted, he braced a leg against the jamb and pulled harder. The result was the same. Glancing at Harkin, he shook his head.

"I don't believe this. Now, of all times!" Harkin stabbed another button on the intercom. "Security, this is Harkin. What the hell is going on?"

Static crackled, then, "Deever here, sir. There's been a primary breach in Lab 22. The first phase of lockdown has been initiated."

Harkin let up on the button and turned toward the military brass. "I apologize for the inconvenience of this false alarm. There can't really be a breach. Our safety procedures are impeccable, our equipment the best on the market. Bear with me for a few minutes and I'll have this sorted out."

Brognola noticed that Harkin didn't address him or anyone else from the intelligence community. It was quite obvious that all Harkin cared about were his hundreds of millions of dollars' worth of Pentagon contracts.

The industrialist turned to the intercom again. "Deever, listen carefully. Are the backup priority emergency circuits functioning?"

"As near as I can tell, sir, yes," came the disembodied reply.

"Excellent. I want you to initiate the manual override sequence and let us out of here. My guests are to be taken to the surface immediately."

"But sir—" Deever sounded uncertain "—if I do that, it will unlock every door below ground level. Including Lab 22. Is that wise?"

"I'll take full responsibility. After you've done it, buzz our people on the surface. Have them get the elevators up and running. Or, at the very least, unlock the door at the top of the stairs. This situation is completely unacceptable."

When there was no immediately replay, Harkin snapped, "Deever? Did you hear me?"

"Yes, sir. But this is Code Red, sir. Even if I could contact topside, which I can't because all the lines are down, the central computer has killed the elevators and there's no manual override for them."

Harkin smacked the glass partition with his fist, then barked, "I refuse to be cooped up a minute longer than I have to. Unlock the doors and get your butt down here on the double. You're to escort us to Sublevel 1."

Brognola felt sorry for the guy at the other end. Working for a man like Luther Harkin had to be a living hell. He looked up at the ceiling when the Klaxons abruptly faded.

"Begging your pardon, sir," Deever hedged, "but what if a biotoxin is spreading through the sublevels even as we speak?"

Harkin gave a start but recovered his composure almost instantly. "That's why biohazard suits were invented. You have several in a storage locker, as I recall. Put one on and get down here. You've stalled long enough."

Lucy Reese stood up. "Hold on, Luther. You're putting his life at risk. You know that, don't you?"

"Ever the flair for dramatics, eh?" was Harkin's rejoinder. "Our biosuits are top of the line. They protect against every type of vector known to man. Airborne, direct contact, you name it."

"Speaking of air, sir," another staffer interjected, "there's none reaching us." She had gone over to a duct and was holding her hand over it. "The ventilation system has been shut down."

Brognola had heard enough. It was time to use his clout to bail them out. Unclipping his cellular phone, he activated it and fed in a special number to mission control at Stony Man Farm. But when he tried to place the call, the display read No Service Area.

Harkin had been watching him. "You can't reach the outside world using that. Cell phones won't work down here. Our facility is shielded to prevent it."

"Let me guess," Lucy Reese said. "You don't want to risk having your precious secrets leak out?"

"You make it sound like a crime," Harkin countered, "when I'm merely protecting my company and my country. If certain foreign powers were able to replicate the substances we design, none of us would be safe."

Bryce Chandler broke his long silence. "How safe are we right now? From the sounds of things, we could use protective gear of our own."

"I'm more concerned about suffocating," Gregory Merton said. "How long will our air hold out?"

Harkin raised his hands. "Gentlemen, please! Don't get all worked up over nothing. When lockdown was initiated, our main computer switched off the central air to prevent the possible spread of infectious agents. At regular intervals, though, it will pump in enough oxygen to sustain life."

"That's encouraging," Reese remarked sarcastically.

"As for protective gear," Harkin went on, "we don't need it at this stage. We're sealed in here as tight as a drum. A pathogen couldn't possibly infect us."

Brognola wasn't so sure. No matter how well constructed, no place was ever airtight. He noticed the lab assistants were having a heated argument and wondered what it was about. He didn't have to wonder for long.

Dr. Bellamy pressed the lab's intercom. "Mr. Harkin,

have you learned where the contamination has taken place?"

"Lab 22."

The scientist took a step back. Behind him, the argument became more heated, and a woman began to cry.

"What the devil is going on in there?" Harkin demanded.

Dr. Bellamy was gazing at the vial in his hand as if afraid it would bite him.

"Haven't you grasped the significance yet?"

"I hate riddles. Enlighten me, and be quick about it."

Demonstrating the patience of a saint, Bellamy elaborated. "Remember our coding system? The identifiers we assign are based on the geographic location of the source material and the laboratory in which the substance was created." He wagged the vial. "BE7722."

"Yes? So?" Harkin responded.

"BE77—22," Bellamy repeated, stressing the last two numbers.

Brognola saw shock take hold of Harkin, and his own unease mounted. "Mind telling us why you look as if you just swallowed a handful of nails?" he demanded.

Harkin pressed his forehead to the glass pane and murmured, "Not that! Of all of them, not that!"

Brognola took over the intercom. "Dr. Bellamy?" he prodded. "What are we missing here? In a nutshell, if you please."

The scientist hesitated.

"Need I point out I'm here as the President's personal liaison?" Brognola played his trump card. "Failure to answer me is the same as failing to answer him, and he won't be happy when he hears of it."

"Hold on!" Harkin roused from his stunned state. "I'll be the judge of what we need to reveal and what we don't. You'll need a more compelling reason for me to let the good doctor break his oath of secrecy."

"Fine," Brognola said. "How about if I recommend to the

President that he have this facility closed indefinitely? Is that compelling enough?"

Radiating spite like the sun radiated light, Harkin nodded at Bellamy, who touched the vial.

"Extracting the derivative is a long and complicated process. BE7722 goes through several stages, or states, before the end result is achieved." Bellamy gnawed on his lower lip. "One of those forms is extremely contagious and volatile."

The guests were listening with great interest. "You make it sound almost like a virus," General Scott of Army Intelligence remarked.

"Only in one sense. At its most potent, the extract can be absorbed through the pores of the skin." Bellamy let them digest that. "It doesn't take much. A drop the size of a pinhead contains enough to do the job."

Brognola cut right to the heart of the matter. "What does it do that has you so worried? Is it lethal?"

"Not directly, no. But those who have been exposed exhibit the most—"

A green light on the wall unit came on. "Hold it!" Harkin commanded. "Security is trying to get through." He switched channels. "Deever? I trust you have good news?"

"I am about to start down, sir." Deever's voice was tinny, almost mechanical. "I'm suited up, and we've patched the suit's mike through the console." From the speaker issued a metallic click. "We've overridden the lockdown, as you ordered, but I suggest you stay where you are until I've verified the coast is clear. Should I report in as needed or keep the com link open?"

"I want a running commentary," Harkin directed. "My guests need to be assured their lives aren't in any danger."

Over his shoulder, he explained, "The security office is on Sublevel 6. Deever can check the status of each floor on his way down. If all is well, as I am confident is the case, we'll be out of here in no time."

Harkin spoke into the intercom again. "Did you hear that, Deever?"

"Yes, sir. I'm opening the security door now. Good thing I've brought a flashlight. It's even darker in the hall. Appears to be deserted. The doors to all the other rooms are shut. I've closed the security door and am now moving past Lab 12. There's no sign of anyone inside."

Harkin glanced at Brognola and the other visitors. "There are two labs on each level, numbered consecutively, along with various offices and whatnot."

Deever's heavy breaths rasped from the speaker. He was nervous and couldn't hide it. "The rec room is coming up. Funny. It's darker than anywhere else. I don't see anyone inside, but I know there were five or six people in there right before the Klaxons went off. I wonder where they got to?"

"Who cares?" Harkin shouted. "Stick to what is important."

Brognola was speculating on how long it would be before any Stony Man personnel became aware of his situation, and what, if anything, they could do about it. Their specialty was gathering intelligence and logistics. Anything and everything having to do with tactical support for Phoenix Force and Able Team. And for Mack Bolan, of course. When it came to biohazards, their expertise was limited.

"I'm proceeding into the stairwell," Deever reported. "It's like a cave in here. Nearly pitch black."

Harkin tried to be helpful in his own inimitable fashion. "Don't trip over your own feet, but hurry it up. I don't want my guests detained here any longer than absolutely necessary."

General Drake spoke for all of them. "We're in no danger at the moment. His safety comes first. Don't rush him on our account."

Deever's breathing grew louder. "I'm descending to the next landing, sir. I shone my light up and down. The stairwell appears to be empty, but I'm sure I heard something. I don't mind admitting my nerves are on edge."

"Don't let your imagination get the better of you," Harkin cautioned. "There had to be people in the corridors when the lockdown was imposed. And now that the doors are open, more are bound to be out and about."

Brognola had a thought. "How many personnel work here?"

"Total?" Harkin responded. "Two hundred and nine. One hundred and sixty-four of those work underground." He smiled. "Everyone was required to be on station today. I wanted to show you Spider Mountain at its best."

A warning bell pinged in Brognola's mind. With numbers like that the security guard should have encountered others by now.

"I'm at the landing to Sublevel 7," Deever said. "Want me to check the corridor?"

"Yes," Harkin instructed.

"It's strange, sir. There's no sign of anyone on this level, either. Should I go from room to room?"

"No. Continue on down the stairwell. Inform me the moment you run into anyone."

"Will do," Deever replied, still sounding nervous.

Tension crackled like electricity. Brognola wasn't the only one hanging on Deever's every statement. Something was wrong, seriously wrong, and everyone was anxious to find out what.

"Sir, did you hear that?" Deever suddenly asked.

Harkin gave a startled response. "Hear what?"

"A cry of some kind. It came from Sublevel 8. I don't know what to make of it. Should I investigate?"

"No. Freeing us takes priority over everything else." Beads of sweat had formed on Luther Harkin's brow. "Don't stop for anything," he ordered.

"Yes, sir." Deever was silent a long while. "I'm at Sublevel 9 now. Still no sign of a living soul. Wait. What's this?"

The VIPs and staffers alike edged toward the intercom, Brognola foremost among them.

"What is it?" Harkin goaded. "Have you found someone?"

"No, just a broken cup and a puddle of spilled coffee on the floor. I'm continuing to Sublevel 10. Another five minutes and I should be outside your door."

"It can't be soon enough," Harkin stated. "I don't like being cooped up."

Neither did Brognola. Which was ironic, since most days he was chained to his desk at the Justice Department or his office at Stony Man.

Harkin snapped his fingers. "One more thing, Deever. When you reach the bottom, check the hazard monitors at the end of this hall. If a biotoxin has been released, they'll show it."

"Copy that, sir." Deever gave a sharp intake of breath. "There's that cry again. It's the damnedest sound, if you don't mind my saying so. Almost like an animal. It's getting closer. Whatever it is, it's below me and climbing."

A staffer raised her arm like a fifth grader trying to get the teacher's attention. "Maybe someone has been hurt, Mr. Harkin, and needs medical attention," she suggested.

Harkin shot her a look that implied she would be the one needing medical attention if she opened her mouth again.

The intercom was silent a few seconds, then suddenly Deever spoke, sounding excited. "I see someone! Several people, in fact! I think one of them is Lafferty, the chemist."

Deever's voice took on a new note—one of budding fear. "They're moving strangely. They must be sick or—" Deever paused. "Good God! It can't be! Keep back! No!" A scream of pure terror crackled from the speaker, followed by horrendous sounds of struggle.

Then there was nothing.

Nothing at all.

4

Stony Man Farm, Virginia

The Executioner knew something was going down the moment he entered the main house. People were scurrying about on errands, and the chief of communications went running by without a word of greeting.

Bolan headed for the elevator and spotted Stony Man's resident weaponsmith, John Kissinger. "What's going on, Cowboy?"

"Beats me, Mack. I was in the armory taking inventory when word came down that Price wants everyone in the War Room ASAP."

The elevator was crammed with support staff. They pressed back as Bolan entered, creating enough room for him and for Kissinger. The door whirred shut.

"For once the gang's all here," Kissinger commented as the car descended smoothly toward the basement. "Usually, either Phoenix, Able or you are off on a mission somewhere."

"I just got back," Bolan told Kissinger.

"When Barb is done with us, you might want to stop by. Some new ordnance has arrived from overseas, including a German submachine gun prototype you might want to try. It's made almost entirely of polymers. So lightweight, it floats." Kissinger grinned.

Bolan always familiarized himself with the latest hardware on the market. He never knew when he might find himself in a firefight against someone using it. "I'll have a look at it first chance I get."

The elevator pinged and Bolan led the exodus. He and Kissinger turned left, past the Gun Room and a couple of offices, to a steel door. Entry was by coded access. He let Kissinger do the honors.

The weaponsmith hadn't exaggerated. Every Stony Man commando was present. So was the primary support crew: Barbara Price; Aaron Kurtzman, the wheelchair-bound computer expert and intelligence guru; Kurtzman's cybernetic wizards, Hunt Wethers, Carmen Delahunt and Akiro Tokaido. At the far end of the big table, slouched in his chair, was Jack Grimaldi. The pilot smiled when he spotted Bolan and raised a hand in greeting.

Bolan slid into an empty chair next to Price. He gave her a polite nod and she returned it.

"Welcome back," Price said to him, then raised her voice for the rest to hear. "Now that we're all accounted for we can begin." She nodded at the clock. "Exactly nine minutes and twenty seconds ago we learned of a crisis situation at the Spider Mountain Research Facility."

"The what?" The question came from Carl Lyons, Able Team's leader.

"A biopharm operation under the umbrella of Harkin Industries," Price said in clarification. But even that wasn't enough.

"What in the world is a biopharm?" Rafael Encizo asked. The Phoenix Force vet was a demon with a blade but when it came to the latest scientific and technological developments, he left the intel to the experts.

"Biopharming is the latest biotechnology craze," Price informed everyone. "It involves genetically modifying plants to make new drugs."

"What kind of drugs?" Hermann "Gadgets" Schwarz

asked. He was Able Team's electronics expert. He could also kill with the stealth and speed of a cobra.

"You name it, they're trying to develop it. Industrial enzymes, allergenic enzymes, contraceptives, vaccines—the works. They use all sorts of plants. Ordinary varieties like rice, corn and barley. And exotics from around the globe. It's been estimated there are upward of three hundred secret biopharming operations in the U.S. alone," Price explained.

"Why secret?" David McCarter asked. "What's the big deal over playing God with the greenery?"

"Industrial profits, for one thing," Price replied. "Breakthroughs can mean big bucks. Imagine how valuable a new vaccine for the West Nile Virus would be. Or for AIDS." She tapped a file in front of her. "Then there are the military applications. Some biopharming is done under the auspices of the Department of Defense."

Jack Grimaldi sat up. "Bioweapons from a corn cob? The mind boggles."

Bolan had detected an undercurrent of anxiety in Price that no one else seemed to have noticed. He cut to the chase. "How does all this tie in with why you called us together?"

"The Spider Mountain Research Facility is a Department of Defense sanctioned biopharm," Price began. "They deal in top-secret projects. Luther Harkin is the CEO. Today he invited some military brass and reps from the intelligence community to a special demonstration. Hal was one of them." She raked them with a hard stare. "We have reason to believe he might be in trouble."

"What can go wrong at a potato farm?" McCarter cracked.

"Let me spell it out." Price became positively somber. "Spider Mountain specializes in the sort of nasty things you wouldn't want to face in the field. Bioweapons. Biotoxins. The whole gamut."

"Hold the phone," Grimaldi said. "I may not be the brightest bulb here, but even I know that the U.S. signed a treaty years ago forbidding the development of biological weapons."

It was Kurtzman who responded. "The problem with treaties is that they always contain loopholes. Yes, we were signatories to that accord. But it only forbids the development of offensive bioweapons. It doesn't prevent us from developing defensive ones."

"I don't see the difference," Calvin James commented.

"We're allowed to do research into bioweapons that might one day be used against us," Kurtzman told him. "That includes coming up with new ones of our own just so we can prepare a defense against them."

Hunt Wethers chuckled. "Circular logic. Gotta love it. A treaty that bans biological weapons yet still lets you make them? How sane is that?"

"Biopharms are subject to strict safety protocols," Price stated. "They must conform to safety guidelines set by the Centers for Disease Control, the United States Department of Agriculture and other agencies."

"The USDA?" Grimaldi found it amusing. "What do they do? Count seeds?"

"Yes, but that's neither here nor there." Price leaned forward. "What matters is that we've been monitoring emergency communications between Spider Mountain, the CDC, the Virginia Department of Emergency Management and the Defense Department. There's been a containment breach and all contact with the outside world has been cut. A Phase One Biotoxin Hazard Alert is in force, and Spider Mountain is being sealed off."

Now Bolan understood her undercurrent of anxiety. "And Hal is still in there?"

"Our intercepts indicate he's underground with the rest of the VIPs, including Luther Harkin himself."

The full gravity of the crisis slowly sank in. Grimaldi said out loud what they were all thinking. "So you're saying the boss might have been exposed to one of those bioweapons you were talking about?"

"There is that possibility, yes." Price's expression was grave.

Bolan's mind was working. Brognola was more than a Fed, more than just their liaison to the Oval Office. He was a friend, a damn good one, and had been there for Bolan more times than the soldier could count.

"What's the government doing to get them out?" he asked Price.

"For the time being, nothing. Not until it can be determined what kind of biotoxin they're dealing with."

"There has to be something we can do," McCarter insisted.

"There are several things," Price agreed. "We can continue to monitor communications going in and out of Spider Mountain. We can dig up intel on the projects they've been working on. We can try to contact Hal. And we might want to consider inserting someone on-site to monitor events. Which means laying our hands on a CDC biohazard suit."

Kurtzman rolled his wheelchair toward the door. "I'll handle the intel end. Hunt, Carmen and Akiro, you're with me."

Cowboy Kissinger stood. "For once I can do more than polish weapons. An old buddy of mine from my Ohio State days has been with the Centers for Disease Control for years. We've kept in touch. I bet he can give me a line on getting hold of that suit you want."

Next to rise was Carl Lyons, and when he did, so did the rest of Able Team. "There's not much we can contribute at this point. Since we've only had about four hours' sleep over the past two days, I think it's best we catch up. If you need us, give a yell." They filed out.

That left Phoenix Force. David McCarter pushed to his feet. "We're not much use, either. But if you want to send us to Spider Mountain to kick some major butt, we're your boys."

Soon Bolan and Price were alone. The soldier leaned back

in his chair, studying her. "What do you rate Hal's chances of making it out alive?"

"I honestly can't say. There are too many unknown factors at this point. But I do know that if a bioengineered pathogen has been released, the odds of his survival become slimmer the longer he's trapped down there." Price scooped up her folder. "I'd better get to the Communications Room."

"One more question," Bolan said. "Why do we need a CDC biohazard suit when we have suits stored here in case of a biological attack on the Farm?"

"The CDC uses a different suit than the kind we have. Ours were funneled from the military. They're not the same color, and they're fitted with options the CDC suits don't have. Whoever we insert on-site has to blend in, so the CDC version is a must."

Bolan sat at the table for a full minute after Price left the room. His forehead was knit in thought. Then he rose and made his way to Kissinger's office. The door was open, and the weaponsmith was on the phone.

"Yes, I understand. But it's urgent I reach him. Can you have him get back to me as soon as the meeting is over? I'll give you my cell phone number." Kissinger did just that, then said politely, "Thank you, Ms. Havershaw," and hung up.

Bolan rapped on the doorjamb. "No luck with your CDC contact?"

Kissinger shook his head. "That was his secretary. He's due back in the next half hour or so."

"Time is of the essence on this one," Bolan remarked.

"Tell me something I don't know." Kissinger sighed. "Did you want to see that prototype I was telling you about?"

"No. I want you to get your hands on two suits."

"How's that?" Kissing was surprised.

"We'll need two biohazard suits. The job will take more than one man," Bolan stated

Kissinger was puzzled and it showed. "What job is that?"

"Getting Hal out alive."

"But Barb didn't say anything about—" Kissinger stopped. "Oh, I see. You realize, I trust, that whoever goes in will be at extreme risk? Much more so than an average mission. You could be committing suicide."

"I'd take it as a favor if you don't say anything to Barb just yet."

"Sure. If you'll do a favor for me."

"Name it," Bolan said.

"When you break the news to her, videotape it. I've never seen a person turn purple before." Kissinger gave Bolan a shaky grin.

THE SPIDER MOUNTAIN Research Facility was at the epicenter of a whirlwind. Units of the Virginia Army National Guard had been brought in, including the 29th Infantry Division and the 34th Civil Support Team. A cordon had been thrown around the perimeter fence, and the Harkin Industries security guards at the main gate had been replaced by the Guard. State police were on hand. So were deputies from the county sheriff's office. The lieutenant governor had arrived, along with a contingent of state officials.

Word had leaked to the media and dozens of reporters were on the scene, with more arriving all the time.

From the air it looked like a three-ring circus. Or so thought Richard Pratt of the Virginia Department of Emergency Management, or VDEM as it was known. The Bell JetRanger helicopter he was riding in banked toward a makeshift landing site south of the facility. Three other copters were already there. Pratt turned to his assistant. "We're the last in, but we carry the most clout, eh?"

Gloria Stenger dutifully smiled. Dressed in a smart business suit, she was the epitome of a professional woman. "As you will show them soon enough, I expect, sir."

Pratt laughed and nudged her elbow. "You can bet your life

I will. This is a career-making opportunity, Stenger. I'm not about to blow it."

"Career-making?" Gloria asked.

Pratt nodded at the bustling beehive of activity. "This is big, Stenger. Monumentally big. By tonight it'll be national news. All the networks will carry it. CNN and FOX will be broadcasting live from the scene. If I handle this right, I'll be the shining star of the hour. Think what that can mean." Pratt was practically glowing with excitement.

The corners of Stenger's mouth tweaked down but her superior didn't notice. "What about the people trapped inside?" she reminded him.

"What about them?" Pratt responded. "We'll do our best to get them out, but I won't lose any sleep if they don't make it. Public welfare and safety come first. Remember your training? The motto you were taught?"

"The greatest good for the greatest number," Stenger recited.

"Exactly. When you're dealing with pathogens with the potential to wipe out the human race, you have to look at the big picture." Pratt patted her arm. "You're new at this. Give yourself time. You'll get the hang of it."

Their pilot positioned the aircraft over a suitable spot and slowly brought them to earth.

Pratt wasn't waiting on ceremony. He was out the door a second later and barreled toward a reception committee, bent low so as not to lose his head to the whirring rotor blades.

Stenger hopped down and hustled to keep up. She had an attaché case in one hand, a laptop in the other, a plastic folder tucked under her left arm and a handbag over her right shoulder. Her boss hadn't offered to carry anything. He never did.

A stately gray-haired gentleman advanced to meet them. "Mr. Pratt? I'm Arthur Roarke, vice president of Harkin Industries. We were told you would be arriving to assess the situation."

Pratt had straightened and was adjusting his tie. "You were

misinformed. I'm not here to assess anything. I'm here to take control as mandated by law. If you have any questions, take them up with my assistant here." Jerking a thumb at Stenger, he moved toward several waiting vehicles.

"The nerve of some people!" Roarke exclaimed, and looked sternly at Stenger. "That man is plain rude."

"He's a man with a mission, that's for sure." Stenger attempted to be diplomatic.

But Roarke wasn't buying it. "He's a man with a broomstick up his ass," he muttered.

Pratt was beside a sedan, impatiently tapping his foot. "Will you hurry up, Ms. Stenger? We don't have all day."

"Coming, sir." Stenger had to remind herself that she wouldn't be working for Pratt forever. Her game plan called for her to transfer to the VDEM's Public Affairs Division and spend the rest of her career at a cushy desk job. Fieldwork hadn't turned out to be to her liking, not when she had to put up with a Neanderthal like Pratt. He'd slid into the front seat, leaving her to open the rear door, shove her gear inside and climb in on her own.

"Bring me up to speed, Captain Ziegler," Pratt directed the driver.

Stenger had never set eyes on the man before, but she knew by his uniform he was with the state police. The VDEM worked closely with them in crises like this.

"Everything is under control, sir," Ziegler relayed. "The CDC people are cooperating fully, and have placed their full resources at your disposal. There's been some squawking from the media over not allowing them access to the facility, and we even caught a couple of reporters trying to sneak over the fence, if you can believe it."

"All they care about is a sound bite for their next newscast," Pratt said derisively. "I'll hold a press conference and set them straight. But we mustn't antagonize them. We have our image to think of." Almost as an afterthought, Pratt asked, "Has contact been established with anyone inside?"

"No, sir. There was a power outage, and from what I understand, most of the systems are still down," the officer replied.

"Oh, well." Pratt shrugged. "Once we establish that a pathogen has definitely been released, whoever is down there becomes expendable."

Stenger couldn't keep silent. "Isn't that a little harsh, sir?"

"*Life* is harsh, Ms. Stenger. While I sympathize with their plight, rescuing them isn't our highest priority. Containing whatever threat exists to the rest of humanity is all you should be concerned with at this point."

"So, essentially, what you're saying is that you've already written them off?" She couldn't believe what she was hearing. "That they might be as good as dead, only they don't know it yet?"

Richard Pratt grinned. "You took the words right out of my mouth."

5

"What the hell is taking them so long?" Luther Harkin asked for the twentieth time in as many minutes. He was pacing back and forth in front of the glass partition. "It's been *hours!* They should have had us out of here long before this!" He was beginning to sound hysterical.

None of his staffers answered. They were huddled in a group, their fear thick enough to pierce with a stiletto.

Hal Brognola didn't blame them. The wait was getting on his nerves, too. He was trying hard not to show it, but his hands were clammy and he had to mop his brow more often than normal. Images of his family continually popped unbidden into his mind. Images of the many tender moments they had shared, and might never share again.

General Drake, ever the consummate Marine, had put up with more crabbing than he was willing to tolerate. "Why don't you sit down and take a load off, Mr. Harkin? You're wearing a rut in the carpet."

"It's my carpet," Harkin snapped. But he stopped pacing and glared at his staff. "Why are you standing there? Why do I pay all of you six figures a year? So you can be next to useless when I need you most? Find a way to contact the surface. Or go find out what happened to Deever. But do *something.*"

"No one is going anywhere until we're sure it's safe," Brognola interjected. "We talked it over and decided to sit tight, remember?"

"The rest of you decided to sit tight. I'm merely honoring your wishes out of the goodness of my heart. Were it up to me, we would be at the surface by now."

"Or dead," Lucy Reese said.

Over in the lab, Dr. Bellamy and his assistants were seated either in chairs or on the floor. The young man who had served as subject of the demonstration, still stripped to the waist, was asleep in the elevated chair. He had become listless and sluggish shortly after bending the bar, and had been largely ignored since the lights had gone out.

Lucy Reese was glaring at Harkin. "Do you know what I like about that man?" she whispered to Hal.

"What?" Brognola took the bait.

"Absolutely nothing. He's the kind who in the old days would sell his mother for body parts. Or fire a secretary for putting too much sugar in his coffee. Or dump a woman who didn't meet his standard of perfection."

At last Brognola had a clue to her hatred. "Since you're too young to be his mother, and you don't strike me as a gofer, I'd say you're the woman behind door number three."

Reese tried to smother a grin and failed. "It was a long time ago. He was an up-and-coming tycoon, and I was a country gal who thought all men were gentlemen and romances always had fairy-tale endings."

Gregory Merton, who until that moment had been slumped in a chair in a funk, suddenly jumped up. "There it is again! Do you hear that? What in the world is it?"

Brognola heard the sound, and it made his skin crawl. From the corridor right outside their door came savage snarls and beastlike roars, as if a menagerie of wild animals was running loose. They had heard it several times before, but never so loud, and never so close.

Over in the lab, Dr. Bellamy stood up, his head cocked. When the bestial bedlam ceased, he stepped to the intercom. "They know we're here. They'll try to break through eventually. And they might well succeed," he said, emanating real fear.

Bryce Chandler walked toward their host. Anticipating a confrontation, Brognola trailed along. His instincts were right on.

"Mr. Harkin," Chandler began pleasantly enough, "I'll give you sixty seconds to tell us what in God's name is going on. Then I start breaking your fingers, one by one."

Harkin mistook the threat for a joke, and laughed. "Be serious," he said. "Men like us shouldn't go around indulging in idle threats."

Brognola had known Chandler a long time, since they were fledgling agents, he with the Justice Department, Chandler with a covert cell within the NSA that specialized in dirty tricks, and dirtier deeds. Chandler was now well past his prime, but an old lion was still a lion, and not to be taken lightly. So Brognola wasn't surprised when his friend seized Harkin's left wrist, gripped a finger and twisted. Not hard enough to break the bone, but hard enough that the industrialist let out a startled yelp.

"Let go of me, damn it!" Harkin tried to pull loose. "What do you think you're doing?"

"I've already made that clear." Chandler twisted a bit more, causing Harkin to grimace and grip his teeth against the pain. "Explanations are called for, and we will have them, or you will need to hire someone to do your nose picking for the foreseeable future."

Lucy Reese laughed with glee. The generals and the admiral started forward, but Brognola waved them off. Admiral Peters seemed intent on intervening anyway until General Drake said something in his ear. The staffers didn't know what to do. Harkin was their employer, but Chandler was a VIP.

"Now, then," Chandler said, steering Harkin to a chair and shoving him into it. "Let's talk, shall we? But I warn you. My patience is wearing thin. If I sense you're lying or you're holding back. you won't like the consequences."

The speaker crackled to life. "Please don't!" Dr. Bellamy beseeched the NSA honcho. "I can answer any questions you gentlemen have."

Luther Harkin didn't know when he was well off. "Don't you dare!" he barked. "Need I remind you again that you've signed a confidentiality agreement, Doctor? Break it, and I'll make your life a living hell."

Brognola's own patience was frayed. It was obvious something was seriously wrong topside. The power had yet to be restored. There had been no effort made to contact them. The air was thin and stale. A potentially contagious biotoxin might have been released. And someone, or something, was roaming the darkened corridors of Spider Mountain and had attacked Deever. They had to get out of there, but they needed information to help them take action. Information Luther Harkin was denying them.

Leaning on the arms of Harkin's chair, Brognola let him have it with both verbal barrels.

"Need I remind *you* that I was invited here today on behalf of the President. Which should give you some idea of the clout I have at the highest level. So believe me when I say that unless you start filling us in, I will use all of my considerable influence to see that Harkin Industries never lands another government contract as long as I live."

Harkin's Adam's apple bobbed. He squirmed and fidgeted like a worm on a hook, then angrily motioned. "Go ahead, Doctor. Tell them whatever they want to hear."

The big Fed and the other guests moved to the partition. "Let's start with the basics. You believe there has been a breach in a lab on the floor above us, I take it? That BE7722 has leaked out?" Brognola began the questioning.

The scientist wearily nodded. "I can't say exactly how. Any number of things could have gone wrong. Maybe the lightning was a factor. Maybe a lab worker was careless. But from the sounds we've heard, from what happened to our security chief, Deever, yes, I'd say it has to be BE7722."

"Be more specific," Brognola directed him.

Bellamy reached into a pocket of his lab coat and once again displayed the vial. "In its refined state, BE7722 is harmless. Injected into the bloodstream, it gives a person the strength and stamina of five men for short periods of time." He indicated the sleeping subject. "The strain on the body is great, however. After the effects wear off, exhaustion sets in."

"And in its unrefined state?" Brognola probed.

"In our early tests, mice and rats turned into raging killers. They would go berserk. If another mouse or rat was placed in their cage, they'd attack and kill it." Bellamy tiredly rubbed his eyes. "Additional experiments showed us that the condition could be passed on by mere physical contact. Or by breathing concentrated vapors from a beaker."

Brognola couldn't see a lab mouse breathing beaker fumes. "How did you find that out? Was one of your people infected?" He made direct eye contact with the scientist.

Dr. Bellamy seemed to age ten years. "Yes," he admitted. "He didn't stick to procedure. The first inkling we had was when he passed out. Coworkers revived him, and when he came to, he raged among them like a madman. Two had to be hospitalized with multiple fractures and wounds."

Bryce Chandler expressed a thought that had popped into Brognola's own mind. "Strange I never heard of this. An incident like that would have made the news. Or, at the very least, been bandied about in intelligence circles."

"We were ordered to keep quiet about it," Bellamy informed them, then added, as if to justify the cover-up, "The man responsible later made a full recovery and we put new safeguards into effect to ensure it never happened again."

Brognola looked at Luther Harkin. "What you did was not only unethical, it was against the law."

"It was a minor occurrence, nothing more," the industrialist said sullenly. "I wasn't going to let it jeopardize our bio-enhancement project. A major scientific breakthrough was at stake."

"Not to mention millions of dollars in your pocket," Brognola said, then turned to the scientist. "Go on, Doctor. Fill us in on what BE7722 does."

"And keep it simple," Gregory Merton demanded. "Too much medical mumbo-jumbo gives me a headache."

"As you wish." Bellamy opened his mouth to say more, but the laboratory door rocked to a resounding blow that caused the lab assistants to jump up in alarm and back fearfully away. Bellamy whirled, the blood draining from his craggy face. "They're trying to break in!" he screamed.

Harkin rose, his twisted finger momentarily forgotten. "Don't panic, Doctor. The doors are made of a plasticine alloy. Even one of those creatures can't break it down."

Brognola was given no time to wonder about the use of the word "creatures." Again the door shook to a powerful blow, and he was amazed to see it shake on its hinges. Simultaneously, from the corridor beyond the lab, came a hideous howl, like a wolf gone rabid. Or a man gone mad.

The lab assistants were backing toward the partition. "What should we do, Dr. Bellamy?" one whined. "We're no match for those things!"

More blows rained on the door, each with the impact of a sledgehammer. Cracks and indentations appeared, clear imprints of human fists. The raw strength required had to be exceptional.

Brognola could only stand and watch. There was no way into the lab from his side of the glass. The blows continued for what seemed like an eternity, all the while accompanied by ferocious snarls and howls. Then, with a last jarring impact, the door buckled, and into the lab lurched a nightmare made real.

PRICE AND KURTZMAN had called another meeting of the senior staff, Phoenix Force and Able Team.

Bolan sat in the same chair as before, his mood as grave as those around him. He did not like what he was hearing.

Barbara Price held the floor. "It's been more than three hours and contact still hasn't been established with those inside the facility. In fact, from what we've gleaned, no attempt is being made to rescue them."

"Why the hell not?" McCarter demanded. "Are the jokers in charge daft or something?"

"Daft, no. Extremely cautious, yes. The Virginia Department of Emergency Management has oversight, and until they know what triggered the lockdown, they refuse to endanger anyone else."

Carl Lyons drummed his fingers on the table. "I can understand wanting to play it safe. But to leave Hal and those other people trapped goes against all reason."

"The man overseeing the operation is playing it strictly by the book. Based on communications we've intercepted, he's in no hurry to send a team down. Bear can fill you in on his background." Price handed over the briefing.

Kurtzman swiveled his wheelchair and read from a file. "Richard Thaddeus Pratt. Single, thirty-eight years of age, worked for the past nine years at the VDEM. Master's degree from Yale. Excellent at his job although his people skills are rated as poor. He's hungry to advance, either to the top spot at the VDEM or over to the CDC or FEMA."

"You'd think he'd want to save everyone," Gary Manning mentioned. "Wouldn't that help his career more than anything else?"

Kurtzman tapped the file. "Pratt has never been a risk taker. He always errs on the side of caution. In this instance, all he has to do is stand on the sidelines and twiddle his thumbs, and he'll still be a hero."

"How do you figure?" Hunt Wethers asked. "Since when is doing nothing heroic?"

"You're a hero if you save countless millions," Kurtzman

said. "Technically, by not risking the spread of a potentially deadly biotoxin, he's doing just that. The media is making him out to be a bureaucratic St. George resisting the evil spread of a bioengineered dragon."

"But surely the President won't stand idly by and let Hal and those others die?" Gadgets asked.

"What's he going to do?" Kurtzman rejoined. "Order the lockdown lifted? What if a biotoxin is released into the general population? It would be the equivalent of political suicide." The computer expert shook his head. "No, if anyone is to get Hal out of there, it has to be us."

Bolan had already figured as much. "How hard would it be?" he asked.

"On a scale of one to ten? I'd give it a twelve." Kurtzman wheeled his chair to a monitor. A computer-generated schematic appeared, a breakdown of the Spider Mountain Research Facility. "As you can see, most of it is underground. Twelve levels, to be exact."

"Knowing our luck," McCarter threw in, "we don't know which one the big guy is on." He chuckled, then saw Price's expression. "Blimey. I was only kidding."

Bolan rose and came around the table to study the breakdown in more depth. "Is there any way in other than by the front door?"

Kurtzman typed on his keyboard, and the schematic enlarged to include an area not previously visible. "There's a utility tunnel. It runs between Sublevel 6 and Annex D, where the backup generators are housed." Again the image changed, showing a small structure south of the main building. "It's bound to be sealed off, but it's the best bet."

Barbara Price had more to contribute. "Before we go rushing off, we need to establish some parameters. This is unlike anything we've ever done. No hostile force is involved."

"What's the big deal?" McCarter said. "We go in, we snatch Brognola, we bring him out. He pats us on the back for a job well done, then sends us off on another mission to get our bloody heads blown off. All just another day in the life of the Stony Man Bunch."

"Do you always look at the bright side?" Price deadpanned. She walked over to the monitor. "This isn't a Colombian drug lord's fortress. We can't blast our way in with C-4. Under no circumstances can we let whatever caused this lockdown to reach the outside world. Millions could die."

Bolan hadn't stopped studying the utility tunnel. "Unless I'm mistaken, access into Sublevel 6 is through an airlock," he said.

"That it is," Kurtzman confirmed. "Similar to a submarine's. It was installed in the event of a scenario just like this. But the airlock itself could be contaminated."

"I won't know until I get there," Bolan stated.

Price wasn't the only one to register surprise. "Why you? Any of the others can do the job just as well," she told him.

"Hal is my friend," Bolan said simply, and turned. "But I can't do it alone. This is a two-man op."

"Pick anyone you want," Carl Lyons stated. "We're with you all the way."

"Got that right," Rafael Encizo declared. "Hal is the foundation of this place. I don't know how well we'd function without him. So who is it going to be?"

Bolan raised a hand and pointed.

"Bloody hell," David McCarter said.

6

Richard Pratt was having the time of his life. He had been interviewed by reporters from all the major media, and his face
was being plastered on every TV screen in the country. The
story had gone national in a big way, just as he had predicted,
and by morning his name would be on everyone's lips as
America's savior.

Pratt had a flair for playing to the cameras. He fed the fears
of the audience by describing in gory detail what could happen should a biotoxin be unleashed. Then he soothed those
fears by vowing to do all in his power to guarantee the unthinkable never occurred.

The reporters ate it up with a spoon. They fawned over Pratt
as if he were a movie star. One squeaky-voiced vixenish reporter had even gone so far as to give him a huge hug and de-
clare on camera, "Thank God for men like Richard Pratt,
America's first line of defense against invisible invaders."

A great line, one Pratt made sure to repeat in subsequent interviews. He only hoped his superiors were watching. In a year
or two he might find himself director of the operations division.

"Isn't it great?" Pratt said to his assistant.

GLORIA STENGER HAD smiled and nodded but deep down she
was in turmoil. While her boss preened like a pampered cat,
nothing was being done about the people trapped below. Oh,
Pratt had made it a point to give the idea of saving them lip

service, but he never gave the order to go in. For that matter, he was doing little to establish contact. So, as he strolled toward the front gate to be interviewed by the BBC, she quietly slipped across the compound to Annex D.

The interior was a charred shambles. Despite being properly grounded, despite circuit breakers, despite every precaution conceivable, most of the circuits and half of the generators had been fried by the lightning strike. The room reeked from the acrid stench of burned insulation.

Three electricians were working diligently to restore the power. "How's it coming?" Stenger asked them.

A portly man wearing a Virginia Tech baseball cap looked up from a pair of wires he was splicing. "Slow as molasses, lady. It would go a lot faster if that boss of yours did as I suggested and brought in some help." He surveyed the ruin. "At this rate, we won't have everything back up and running until the middle of next week."

"What about the telephones?" she wondered aloud.

The electrician jerked a thick thumb at a fourth worker she hadn't noticed. There was a big, bearded fellow on his knees in front of a junction box. "Talk to the phone guy. But don't get your hopes up."

The junction box was a mess, too. Wires and terminals had melted like so much wax, and even Stenger could tell it would take a lot of time and effort to get the phones and all of the related systems up and running again. "Sorry to bother you. I'm from the VDEM. Can you give me some idea of when I'll be able to talk to the people below?" she asked hopefully.

The man didn't look up. "Next Christmas," he mumbled.

"I'm serious," she said.

"So am I, lady. You have eyes, haven't you? The bolt that did this could have knocked out an entire city. I've been with the phone company pretty near twenty years, and I've never seen worse." He snipped a burned wire. "I guess this is what happens when you tick off the Almighty."

"I don't follow you."

"God, lady. The guy upstairs. Maybe you've heard of him? And five will get you ten He's not too happy about us lowly mortals meddling where we shouldn't." He glanced at her for the first time. "I've heard a little about what goes on in this place. Tampering with nature, is what it is. Meddling where we shouldn't. Playing God. And God doesn't like it."

Stenger had a retort about superstitious nonsense on the tip of her tongue, but she swallowed it. She needed his cooperation, not his animosity. "I've always been leery of bioengineering myself. But that's not the issue here. There are people trapped down there, and we need to do our best to bring as many of them out alive as we can. Agreed?" she pleaded.

"I suppose." The man didn't sound all that enthused.

"All I need is one line. Can you give me that much? Any office, any lab, will do. Just so I can find out how bad off they are." Stenger placed a hand on his shoulder. "Will you do it as a personal favor to me?" She smiled her best smile.

The guy scratched his beard, then took a pair of needle-nose pliers from his toolbox and lightly pried at several wires set a few inches apart from the rest. "You see these?" he said. "They're secure lines to the security post, and they're not as bad as the rest. I might be able to get one working."

"That would be wonderful."

She decided not to mention it to Pratt just yet. She would make contact, then inform him.

"Don't get your hopes up, lady. Even if we do get through, there might not be anyone to answer. They could all be dead, for all we know," the phone man reminded her.

"Thank you for trying anyway." Stenger headed for the rear, down an aisle flanked by generators. A young Virginia National Guardsman lounging near a circular metal access hatch spotted her and stood straight, one hand on the strap of the M-16 slung over his shoulder.

"Any signs of life, Private?" Gloria asked hopefully.

"No, ma'am. It's been quiet as a tomb since that bunch from the CDC and those Department of Emergency Management folks got done testing the air and such." The soldier glanced at the airlock. "They say it's safe. But I'll feel a heap better once my shift ends."

"If you hear any unusual sounds, you're to come get me right away. I'm at the command post in Annex A, near the front gate. Got that?" Stenger ordered the young soldier.

"I'd like to oblige, ma'am. The only thing is, I'm not supposed to leave my post under any circumstances," he said. "The colonel himself gave me that order, and I'm not about to tick him off."

Stenger indicated a walkie-talkie clipped to his belt. "Then contact your colonel and have him send someone else. I need to know the moment you hear anything. It's vitally important."

The young guardsman smiled. "You can count on me, ma'am."

She hoped so. "Just be sure word is relayed to me personally. Understood?" Pratt would throw a fit if he found out she was conniving behind his back to do what he should be doing.

As she emerged from the building, Stenger was bathed in the spotlight from a helicopter hovering over the south fence. In bold letters on its side were the letters NBC. A cameraman was leaning out of the bay, filming. She was tempted to flip him the finger but instead she smiled sweetly and returned to Annex A.

"Where the hell have you been?" Pratt demanded. "You're not supposed to go traipsing off on your own without informing me."

"Your interview with the BBC is over already?" She evaded the question.

"I had to cut it short," Pratt said dourly. "I got a call from the governor. He's on my case to speed things up. To contact the people trapped below as quickly as feasible." Pratt frowned. "From a comment or two he made, I think someone is putting pressure on him."

"Does this mean you'll bring in more workers so we can restore power sooner?"

Pratt wasn't paying attention. He was staring off into space. "Who would have that kind of pull? I wonder." Shaking himself, he picked up a sheet of paper from a desk he had commandeered. "Something else strange is going on. Have you taken a look at this?"

It was the list of people sealed below when the lockdown was implemented. "What about it?" Stenger asked. "I counted 164 names."

"A footnote at the bottom of the second page mentions eight visiting VIPs, but it doesn't list who they are. I checked with Harkin Security but they have no record, either."

"Mix-ups happen," Stenger said.

"This seems more in the nature of a cover-up than a mix-up, and I don't like it. It complicates things. Anyone powerful enough to pressure the governor isn't someone I want to tick off." Pratt leaned back in his chair. "Contact Virginia Power. I want them to send every available repairman they have."

Thank God, Stenger thought. Out loud she said, "You know best, sir."

HAL BROGNOLA THOUGHT he had seen it all. Junkies strung out on the hard stuff, crackheads who turned into raging lunatics. But he had never beheld anything like the appalling apparition that shambled into Lab 24.

It was a man in a white lab coat, but all semblance of humanity was missing. He walked with a stiff-legged shuffle, his body twitching and convulsing, his fingers clenching and unclenching like the claws of a cat. His teeth were bared, his face a mask of primal savagery. Over his lower lip oozed a continuous stream of drool. But it was his eyes that unnerved Brognola the most. As wide as half-dollars, lit by a maniacal gleam, they were so bloodshot they blazed red, like the eyes of some demon.

The man's hands were bleeding profusely, his knuckles

split, a finger splintered from his assault on the door, but he did not appear to have noticed.

Dr. Bellamy and the others were transfixed with stark terror. The intercom was on, and Brognola heard the scientist whisper, "No one move or speak!"

A female assistant chose that moment to scream. In the blink of an eye, the red-eyed abomination whirled and sprang. Moving with uncanny speed, the man was on her before she could take a step. His hands wrapped around her neck, throttling off another outcry. Bellamy and two helpers rushed to her aid, but they were much too slow. The crazed man gave a violent wrench, and the woman's spine broke with an audible crack.

"Good God!" Lucy Reese cried out.

Bellamy and his helpers grabbed the man's arms, but with a guttural growl he flung them off like rag dolls.

"We've got to help them!" General Drake declared.

"How?" Brognola watched in helpless dismay as the red-eyed killer lunged at another assistant, raised his struggling victim clear over his head and brutally dashed him to the tiled floor. The assistant's skull split like an overripe melon, spilling brains and gore.

General Drake suddenly grabbed a chair and swung it at the partition. The chair bounced off without leaving so much as a small crack.

Over in the corner, a member of Harkin's personal staff had doubled over and was retching.

Bellamy scrambled to his feet. "We have to get out of here!" he shouted at his three remaining helpers. He turned toward the door and froze.

Another red-eyed figure had appeared. A woman this time, her face contorted, her chin and neck slick with saliva. Her red eyes were focused on Bellamy, who addressed her in a calm, soothing tone, "Rachel, it's me, George. You've been exposed to BE7722. Fight it, Rachel. Resist the adrenaline pumping through your veins."

It did no good. The woman hissed and flew at him.

Bellamy raised his arms to protect his neck and head, only to have both his wrists seized. Rachel spun him, exhibiting the same superhuman strength as the man. She bodily hurled Bellamy against a wall. Bones crunched, and Bellamy sagged like a limp rag.

"We've got to do something!" General Scott shouted, pounding the partition in frustration. "Those berserkers must be stopped!"

The male "berserker," as Scott called them, spun toward the partition. He started moving toward it but stopped when the remaining assistants made a break for the hallway. He was on them in a blur, his assault as fearsome as a tiger's. Two went down in twice as many seconds. The last, a panic-stricken woman, managed a few more strides. But the female berserker reached her before she could clear the doorway, and down she went, the berserker's teeth shearing into her throat.

General Scott was nearly beside himself. "Damn, damn, damn!" he raged, pounding the partition.

"Will you cut that out!" Gregory Merton cried. "They'll hear you!"

True enough, both berserkers spun and stalked toward the barrier, their fingers clenching and unclenching, their eyes crimson pools of insanity.

Brognola was sure they would try to break through. The feat seemed impossible, but so had busting down the door. He shouldn't forget their sinews were endowed with five times their natural strength.

With the same ferocity the pair had attacked their victims, they now attacked the partition. Their savagery was startling to behold; raw, elemental, unbridled. The glass shook to the impact.

"I don't get it," Chandler said. "Why don't they go after each other?"

The female was directly in front of Brognola. He detected

no trace of intelligence in her awful red eyes, no hint of the human being she had once been. Instinctively, he backed away, and happened to glance at Luther Harkin.

The industrialist wasn't the least bit interested in the berserkers. He was staring at his watch, grinning.

"What are you so happy about?" Brognola asked.

"Soon it will be four hours since lockdown went into effect," Harkin replied.

Four hours of sheer hell, Brognola thought, as the berserkers redoubled their efforts. He wasn't a pessimist, but something told him the worst was yet to come.

Washington, D.C.

THE MAN WAS TALL and well built. His brown hair had been clipped in a military style crew cut, and his mustache was neatly trimmed. The office in which he sat was Spartan by most standards, a reflection of the man himself. He watched the television a minute longer, then snatched up a telephone and tapped in a number.

"Burt Anderson here," a voice said on the other end of the line.

"This is Tanner. Have you been keeping up with the news?"

"Yeah. FOX just aired a special report. Once I heard he was involved, I expected you to call." Anderson talked in clipped, precise tones, typical of a former Ranger. "What are we going to do?"

"What else can we do?" Tanner asked. On the wall across from his desk hung the bronze logo of the company they had founded: EXECUTIVE PROTECTION, INCORPORATED. "He's had us on retainer for two and a half years. It's time we gave him what he's paid for. I'll call Sax and Romero and have them meet us at the airport. Say, in an hour."

"Hold on a second," Anderson said. "I'm not so sure we should jump on this. He signed a standard contingency contract. We step in only if he's kidnapped or there's a threat against his life."

"You don't think this qualifies?" Tanner ladled on the sarcasm.

"Our contract specifically states the threat must be from hostile parties known or unknown, not some damn virus or germ."

"You're quibbling over the fine print." Tanner opened a drawer and placed a document on the desk. "I was reading his contract earlier, and I have it right in front of me. Let me read one of the clauses."

"I know what it says. I helped write it, remember?"

Flipping to the second page, Tanner ran a forefinger down the margin. "Ah. Here it is." He paused. "Section three, paragraph five. It is further agreed that if the client has not been heard from for a period of four hours, EPI shall initiate a locate-and-retrieve operation."

"Now who's quibbling over the fine print?" Anderson argued. "That clause applies to a suspected kidnapping. And his company must notify us he has vanished. Have they done that? No. Because they know where he's at. So the clause is invalid."

"You're not grasping the total picture," Tanner said. "He's the most high-profile client we have, and one of the most powerful men in the country. Think of how grateful he will be. Think of the feather in our cap. Most of all, think of the waiting list we'll have for new clients wanting to sign on."

"Think of us as slabs in a morgue. Or of the Feds throwing us behind bars for ten years."

"If we do the job right, they'll never even know we were there," Tanner said. "And those biogerms or whatever the hell they're called won't be a problem. I can get my hands on four gas masks on short notice."

"The idea is insane," Anderson said.

"Can I take that as a yes?"

"I hate you." Burt Anderson sighed. "But I won't waste my breath arguing. The airport in an hour?"

"Make it an hour and a half." Tanner hung up and went into the next room. He opened a large closet, slid the jackets and coats aside, and gripped a recessed handle. All it took was a sharp tug for him to lift the panel out, revealing a second, secret closet behind the first. On the right were racks of guns, the whole gamut, from SMGs to rifles to autopistols to revolvers. Underneath were drawers full of ammunition. On the left were other tools of the executive protection trade: glass fiber knives, batons, stun guns, OC spray, body armor and more.

Tanner selected an MP-5 and placed it in a duffel bag. He added ammo, spare clips, a flashlight and a dozen other items. Zipping the bag, he backed out, secured the secret compartment and strode to the door. As he shut it behind him, he grinned and said out loud, "Luther Harkin, here we come."

7

From out of the south streaked a civilian helicopter, a Hughes 500D. Emblazoned on its fuselage were the call letters WKES. The pilot, a tall, lanky man in a blue flight suit, was humming "Flight of the Valkyries." He twisted in his seat when one of his passengers tapped him on the shoulder.

"Are we about there?" Mack Bolan asked.

"Any minute now," Jack Grimaldi said. "From what I hear, the place is a madhouse. We should be able to slip in without anyone noticing."

As if on cue, the copter crested a rise and the Spider Mountain Research Facility blossomed in the night like a spectacularly gaudy flower. The entire top of the mountain was lit up like the White House Christmas tree by huge spotlights. Scores of vehicles were parked on the sides of the road, and many more had pulled off into adjacent fields. A considerable crowd was gathered near the main gate. Overhead, three or four helicopters buzzed like giant bumblebees.

"What did I tell you?" Grimaldi said. "We'll fit right in."

Seven more copters were on the ground. So was a military chopper, sitting apart from the rest.

"Set us down," Bolan directed the pilot.

"Will do, Sarge." Grimaldi moved the stick, and they dipped toward the ground. "This is kind of a switch, isn't it? Us going on a mission with no hardware to speak of and no unfriendlies to deal with."

"I'm sure the agencies overseeing the decontamination won't be too friendly if they find out what we're up to," Bolan observed.

The only weapon he brought along was a Beretta 93-R, snug in a shoulder holster under his left arm. He saw no need for more firepower, not when all they had to worry about were genetically manipulated microbes.

"You know, if you ever start looking at the bright side of things, the shock will kill me." Grimaldi brought the Hughes in over the landing area and positioned it between two news copters, screening them from prying eyes as they landed. "We've arrived on the ground floor. Ladies' lingerie is on the right, jewelry and the wig department on the left."

Bolan indulged in a rare smile, then bent over a long canvas bag at his feet. In bold block letters on both sides were the letters CDC. To its right was another, at the feet of David McCarter. "You've been unusually quiet," Bolan said. The Briton hadn't said three words since they left the Farm.

"This isn't exactly my cup of tea, mate," McCarter responded. "Give me an enemy I can shoot, not one so small I can't see it without a microscope."

"That's not what's bothering you."

"Taken up psychiatry, have you?" McCarter glanced over at Grimaldi, then quietly asked, "Why me, Mack? Carl is better at following orders. Gary is a straight arrow. Some of the others about worship the ground you walk on. I'm just curious as to why you chose me."

"Why not you?" Bolan opened his canvas bag. "Maybe I thought you were the one I most needed at my back," he said.

"Well, your idea of a night on the town leaves a lot to be desired." McCarter bent toward him. "I'd really like to know what skills you think I have that qualify me for this mission."

"You want a list?" Bolan ticked them off on his fingers. "You're not afraid to think for yourself. You're great at improvising, at getting out of tight spots. You imitate accents bet-

'ter than anyone else on Phoenix Force or Able Team. And you read *Scientific American* every month."

McCarter's confusion was almost comical. "Back up a bit. Why is my subscription to a magazine so important? I'm no scientist."

"But you can come across like one if you have to. You know enough jargon to make it sound authentic."

"And my mimicry?"

"The CDC is based in Atlanta, Georgia. You're good at a Southern accent, which will lend extra credibility."

"I'll be damned." A slow smile of open admiration spread across the Briton's rugged features. "You had this all thought out before you told Barb you were going in after Hal, didn't you?"

Bolan didn't answer. He was carefully pulling a CDC biohazard suit from his bag. Proper procedure called for a scrub suit to be worn underneath it, but they both had blacksuits on and would keep them on for the duration. The bag also contained a pair of latex inner gloves and foot covers, but Bolan dispensed with those and began to pull on the biohazard suit.

McCarter imitated him, saying, "Bright blue, eh? One thing about working for our boy Hal. I never know what indignity will be heaped on me next."

Bolan removed the Powered Air Purifying Respirator from the bag. It went around his waist. He tightened the belt so it was snug, then secured a battery to the belt and plugged the battery into the PAPR. He made sure the air hose was over his shoulder and not under his arm.

Grimaldi had switched off the rotors and was scanning the area. "Take your time, fellas. No one is anywhere near us."

Bolan zipped up the suit as high as his neck. He donned the protective hood, positioning the faceplate so his vision wasn't obstructed, then tucked the inner hood liner into the suit and turned on the PAPR. To experiment, he extended both arms, testing his freedom of movement. "Not bad," he said.

"Speak for yourself," McCarter said. "I feel like a ruddy blue Popsicle."

"But it goes great with your complexion," Grimaldi remarked. "You should wear it to the next formal ball at the Farm."

"Were you born bonkers or have you worked at it?" the Briton asked.

Stony Man's ace pilot flourished a pair of identification badges. "Don't forget these. Without them, they won't let you step foot through the gate." He looked at one and held it out to Bolan. "Here you go, Dr. Stephen Brown of the National Center for Infectious Diseases." He looked at the badge again. "What's this 'National Center' stuff?"

McCarter answered. "The CDC is made up of a dozen organizations, not just one." He grinned. "Don't you Yanks know anything about your own country?"

"I know that Barbara said your ID should be enough to make everyone here jump through hoops." Grimaldi read the badge aloud. "Dr. Harrington Clancy of the Office of the Director. Sounds impressive."

"Harrington Clancy?" McCarter repeated, and groaned.

Bolan opened the copter door. "Let's get this show on the road."

FOR ALMOST HALF an hour the bioenhanced research staffers had assaulted the glass partition, pounding their fists against it again and again and again. They never seemed to tire, never seemed to feel the pain they inflicted on their hands and arms. Living automatons, their red eyes bored into those on the other side.

"God, they give me the creeps," Lucy Reese commented at one point.

Hal Brognola had tried the phone to verify there was no dial tone. He had braced a chair against the corridor door to slow down anyone who tried to get at them from that direction. He had stood on another chair and tried to push up a ceiling panel, but it refused to budge. They were truly and utterly trapped.

The others shared his growing sense of desperation.

Bryce Chandler was pacing. Lucy Reese was roving the room for the umpteenth time, seeking a means to escape that didn't exist. The military brass were working on the air vent, trying to pry the grate off with keys and their fingernails. The staffers were nervous wrecks. Several kept trying their cell phones even though they knew the phones wouldn't work. One woman was crying.

Only Luther Harkin was calm. Only Harkin showed no fear, no anxiety. Brognola had been watching him, and he found it distinctly odd that every few minutes the industrialist checked his watch, then grinned, as if at a private joke.

"Look!" Gregory Merton suddenly roared. "Dr. Bellamy is still alive!"

Sure enough, the scientist's right arm was moving, his eyelids fluttering. His chin rose but dropped again.

"What if those things notice?" a staffer asked, aghast.

"Quit calling them that." General Drake had turned from the grate. "They're people, just like us."

Harkin shook his head. "That's where you're wrong. They've lost the capacity to think. To do anything but kill. They're no more human than a bear or a tiger, and they're far more deadly."

"Why?" Admiral Peters wanted to know. "What in God's name has that hellish biosubstance done to them?"

"You'd have to ask the good Dr. Bellamy," Harkin responded. "He's the expert. He once compared its effects to that of PCP."

General Scott balled his fists. "And you wanted to inject that garbage into our troops?"

Brognola didn't blame him for being angry. In high enough doses, PCP had a severe effect. Users couldn't think straight, couldn't concentrate, could barely talk. Worse, raging paranoia set in, and they were prone to incredible acts of violence. Their muscles contracted, and their bodies jerked and twitched like puppets on strings. Exactly as the infected people in the lab were doing.

Harkin pointed at the crazed male. "Do you honestly believe I'd want to turn our soldiers into those slavering freaks? Where's the profit in that? You saw the demonstration earlier. In its refined state, BE7722 doesn't have any adverse side effects."

The mention of the demonstration jarred Brognola like the stab of an ice pick. In all the confusion and excitement they had forgotten about the volunteer, who was still dead to the world in the special chair. The man hadn't stirred once the whole time the rampagers were pounding on the partition. Brognola mentioned as much.

"It's nothing to worry about," Harkin assured them. "Extreme exhaustion is a byproduct of the bioenhancer. It's the one glitch we haven't worked out of the formula yet. But we will."

"If that man wakes up, those horrors will rip him to pieces," Bryce Chandler commented.

The living engines of destruction were still at it. Their hands and forearms were streaked with blood. A shattered bone jutted from the man's left hand, and the woman's knuckles were scraped bare. Yet they wouldn't stop.

Brognola shuddered to think what would happen if they broke through. He was glad there were only two of them. The thought had hardly crossed his mind when another red-eyed mockery shambled into the lab, followed moments later by a second, and then a third. Without a pause they trudged to the partition and added their chemically increased strength to that of the pair already there.

"We're in trouble," Gregory Merton said.

The pounding swelled in volume, thundering in the room's confines. A female staffer screamed.

Brognola knew sooner or later something had to give.

"It's cracking!" a staffer suddenly screeched.

Hairline fractures formed, radiating rapidly outward. In rising consternation Brognola saw the cracks widen, saw their number increase until the partition resembled a spiderweb. Everyone else was backing away and he did the same, grabbing a chair to use in self-defense. The generals and the admiral liked the idea and helped themselves to chairs of their own.

"What can we do? What can we do?" the hysterical woman wailed. Tearing at her hair, she ran in circles, blubbering incoherently.

Luther Harkin checked his watch again. "If only they had a little more time!" he declared.

"Who?" Brognola asked, but received no reply.

Sensing they were on the verge of success, the red-eyed devils howled and keened like a pack of wolves. A cracking sound broke out, growing louder by the moment.

Brognola had seldom felt so helpless. He dearly wished he had a weapon. While he wasn't in the same league as Bolan, or a commando like the dedicated veterans on Phoenix Force and Able Team, he was a fighter by nature. He refused to go down without a struggle.

Pieces of the partition were breaking off and rattling to the lab floor. A hole appeared, small at first, but it widened rapidly. A madman clawed at it, not noticing that in the process he shredded his own fingers.

The generals and the admiral moved between the huddled staffers and the soon-to-be-breached barrier. Grimly, they raised their chairs overhead. "We'll try to hold these things off long enough for the rest of you to escape," General Drake proposed.

Brognola placed himself next to the Marine. "We stand a better chance if we stick together."

Bryce Chandler planted himself on their right. Lucy Reese and two male staffers came over, but the rest were too scared. They retreated to the far wall. The hysterical woman was on her knees, praying at the top of her lungs.

Luther Harkin had mysteriously vanished. Brognola couldn't spot him anywhere. He was about to check again when a tremendous crash heralded the shattering of the partition.

Almost immediately, the berserkers surged forward, growling and snapping. They were incredibly fast when they wanted to be. In a split second they covered the intervening space. The female with the shredded knuckles sprang at General Drake, and was met in midair by Drake's chair. It sent her tumbling, but she was back up again in a flash. Snarling, she renewed her assault.

Brognola had problems of his own. A male attacker charged him. He managed to sidestep, but a backhand caught him across the shoulder and he was hurled a dozen feet to the floor. Excruciating pain lanced his shoulder and chest. It felt as if he had been struck by a sledgehammer. Dazed, expecting the chemically spawned madman to close in for the kill, he rose to his hands and knees.

But the man had barreled straight into the group of petrified staffers and had one by the throat, literally wringing the man's neck. Others tried to slip past and reach the lab, but a pair of drooling grotesqueries cut them off.

Screams, curses and howls added to the bedlam. Brognola gained his feet in time to spot Luther Harkin. The industrialist had been hiding under a row of chairs. He scrambled out from under them and sped into the lab, past the stirring form of Dr. Bellamy and on into the corridor.

Brognola turned to find the chair he had dropped and discovered it was too little, too late. The staffers had been slaughtered and lay in swiftly spreading scarlet pools. The creatures were bent over them, rending and ripping the bodies in grisly abandon.

Admiral Peters was down, his neck mangled. General Winfield had a gaping cavity where his throat had been and was flopping about like a beached flounder. General Drake and General Scott were still fighting. But as Brognola turned toward them, Scott's right arm was torn from its socket.

"Run!" Drake yelled. "Save yourselves if you can!" Two berserkers tried to grab him, and he swung a chair to keep them at bay.

Bryce Chandler and Lucy Reese were almost to the lab. Chandler was limping badly, Reese doing her best to support him.

For a moment Brognola was torn between helping the Marine and helping them. Then Drake went down, a berserker's teeth deep in his neck. Brognola's decision was made for him. He dashed over to Chandler, adding his arm to Reese's.

They passed what was left of the partition. Glass crunched underfoot as they raced toward the corridor. A glance back showed Brognola two figures tearing at General Drake. The other three were converging on a person cowering in a far corner.

Gregory Merton had his arms over his head and was whimpering and crying like an infant. He made no attempt to flee, no effort to defend himself.

There was nothing Brognola could do. He didn't dare yell for Merton to get out of there or the berserkers might hear and come after them. He started to pass the elevated chair. Suddenly the young man in it leaped up, scaring Reese, who nearly tripped over her own feet.

"Let me help. My name is Wells. Tim Wells." He brushed Reese aside.

"You've been awake this whole time?" Brognola guessed.

"Since that brute began pounding on the glass," Wells admitted. "But I didn't want to draw its attention so I played possum…"

"Keep going," Brognola said.

He darted to Dr. Bellamy. The scientist was up on one elbow. Blood trickled from a corner of his mouth and down over his chin. "We have to get you out of here," the big Fed whispered.

Bellamy tried to say something and coughed. More blood oozed out. He took a deep breath and croaked, "Flee while you can! I'm busted up inside. I won't be able to keep up."

Brognola boosted him to his feet. "We're not leaving you." The scientist was the only one who could tell them exactly what they were dealing with.

From the VIP lounge came a shrill whine that ended in a gurgle. Merton's cowardice had ended the only way it could.

Reese, Chandler and Wells made it out the door. Brognola wasn't far behind, Bellamy slumped against him, too weak to stand on his own. Brognola looked up and halted just in time to avoid colliding with the others, who had inexplicably stopped. "What's the matter?" he demanded, then saw the answer for himself.

At the far end of the hall was another infected worker.

8

The National Guardsman at the front gate examined their credentials and promptly allowed them to enter. Bolan let McCarter lead the way since, technically, the Briton was his superior. The generator building was their target, and for a few seconds Bolan thought they would reach it without incident.

"Hold it right there!"

Richard Pratt was stalking toward them. Bolan had seen the man's photo at Stony Man Farm, along with that of Pratt's assistant, Gloria Stenger, who trudged at Pratt's heels. Barbara Price had pulled their files when she learned they were in charge of the overall operation.

"Where did you two come from?" Pratt demanded. "I wasn't aware the CDC was sending anyone else."

McCarter straightened, scowling through his faceplate, and replied in a slight Southern drawl, "Since when is the director of the CDC required to report his every decision to you, Mr. Pratt?"

Pratt drew up short. "I thought our agencies were working together on the decon and containment. Who are you, anyway?"

McCarter flashed his ID. "The director sent us to assess the situation. Word has reached him you're not doing all you should to expedite the recovery of those trapped below."

Bolan had to hand it to the Briton. As the old saying had it, the best defense was always a good offense. Putting the

VDEM administrator on the defensive gave McCarter a psychological edge.

"Where did you hear that?" Pratt asked. " I assure you I'm following procedure to the letter, and doing all in my power that can be done."

"Oh really?" McCarter's skepticism was an indictment in itself. "Then explain to me why you haven't made contact when it's been almost five hours since lockdown."

"Surely you've heard about the power outage? The lightning?" Pratt jabbed a thumb at Stenger. "Update him on the steps we've taken."

"More electricians and a phone crew are on their way," Pratt's assistant revealed.

"We would like to see the extent of the damage for ourselves," McCarter said. "The director wants to hear from me as soon as possible."

A strange look came over Richard Pratt's face. "Is someone putting pressure on him from higher up? That's it, isn't it?"

Bolan had no idea what Pratt was referring to, but McCarter cleverly pounced on the tidbit.

"Did you honestly think a crisis of this magnitude wouldn't be watched closely by the chief executive? He doesn't want a disaster on his hands. The American people have long memories at election time." McCarter paused. "I sure wouldn't want to piss him off. Not if you value your career."

Pratt digested that for a moment. "I'll tell you what. Why don't I have Ms. Stenger give you a tour? She can fill you in on the steps we've taken and answer any questions you might have."

Bolan would have preferred they go alone but knew that to refuse might arouse suspicion.

McCarter apparently realized the same thing, because he smiled and nodded. "That would be fine. Thank you. I'll be sure to mention how well you have cooperated when I talk to the director."

"This way, gentlemen." Stenger moved briskly toward

Annex D. "All the buildings have been checked and re-checked. Decontamination procedures have been followed to the letter, and a decon zone has been established."

"All very commendable," McCarter said. "But your main objective should be rescuing those caught underground."

"I have a man working on a phone link, but he can't give me a definite repair time. We've tried cell phones, but the sublevels are shielded."

Bolan decided to contribute. "Why not lower a microphone down an elevator shaft and see what it picks up?"

"Hard to do without risking contamination," Stenger said. "Our biodetection instruments tell us the shafts are clear, but opening one will cause an updraft, and we don't want that."

"What would you recommend, then?" McCarter asked.

"Were it up to me, I'd have sent someone down hours ago. Almost two hundred lives are at risk. We owe it to them to do all we can to get them out."

"Our thoughts exactly," McCarter told her, and received a grateful smile.

THE WORKERS in the generator building were too engrossed to notice their arrival. Gloria Stenger guided them to a bearded man hunkered in front of a junction box, a portable phone to his ear. A pair of alligator clips had been clamped to wires he had partially stripped. As they watched, he removed a red alligator clip and switched it to a different wire. He grunted, then turned. "Here you are! I was just about to give you a holler, lady, like I promised."

"You have a line working?" Stenger asked, sounding hopeful.

"I'm not sure what we have. I thought I got through to the security station on Sublevel 6. Had to let it ring fifteen times before someone picked up." The repairman paused. "Or I thought someone did."

"Let me hear," Stenger said eagerly. She pressed the portable phone to her ear and listened intently. Confusion blossomed on her face. "What in the world? What do you make of it?"

"Beats me," the repairman said.

Bolan had to hear for himself. Stripping off his hood, he said, "Do you mind?"

The racket at the other end made no sense. He heard growling, punctuated by screaming or maybe even howling in the background. Soon both ceased and were replaced by heavy breathing.

"Is someone there?" he asked.

Through the receiver came a series of snarls and roars, like a bobcat gone amok. Bolan was willing to swear, though, that the vocal cords making the sounds were human. They were so loud, the others heard.

"Do you think they have some Dobermans or German shepherds down there?" the repairman speculated.

Stenger snapped her fingers. "I never thought of that! Harkin Security must use them as watchdogs."

Bolan doubted it. Kurtzman's team had dug up everything on Spider Mountain from blueprints to personnel records, and nowhere in the Harkin Security Division file was there a mention of guard dogs. Still, he supposed there could be a few.

"Thanks," Bolan said. He gave the phone to Stenger and donned his hood again.

Stenger handed it to the repairman, who listened a few more moments, then commented, "Somebody better get down there and feed them or they're liable to turn vicious."

McCarter tapped Stenger on the shoulder. "We'd like to inspect the utility airlock, if you would be so kind."

"It's sealed as tight as a metal drum," Stenger assured them. "Your own people went over it with the newest rapid microbiology testing equipment for plant pathogen detection. But come with me."

A young National Guardsman was next to the airlock, imitating a board. He smiled shyly at Stenger. "There hasn't been a peep from the other side, ma'am."

Bolan peered through a small rectangular window at the interior. "Would you say the inside of the airlock is contamination free, then, Ms. Stenger?"

"I'd stake my life on it," she said. "I offered to don a biosuit and go in, but my boss vetoed it. He wasn't lying when he said he's playing this strictly by the numbers."

David McCarter laid the bombshell on her tactfully. "What would you say if I told you we would like to go in? Right here and now?"

Stenger looked at each of them. "On whose authority? Pratt would have a cow. We do have oversight here, you know."

"Pratt wouldn't need to know," McCarter suggested. "We can be in and out in less than an hour. It's the only way to learn how those underground are faring."

"And if a biotoxin has been released?" Stenger said. "You'll be stuck in quarantine like everyone else. Or worse."

"That's a gamble we are willing to take." McCarter bestowed his most charming smile. "We think lives are more important than red tape. But don't worry. We're not out to endanger anyone topside."

Stenger bit her lower lip. "I don't know. This is all so unexpected. You're either two of the bravest souls I've ever met, or you're nuts."

"Weren't you the one who said we owe it to the people down below to do all we can?" Bolan pressed her. "If you were down there, wouldn't you want someone to come to your rescue sooner rather than later?"

McCarter tried another angle. "We'll never let on that you were a party to it, if that's what is bothering you. No one will ever know besides us three." He glanced at the National Guardsman. "And our young friend here, of course."

Aware all eyes were on him, the young man fidgeted. "My orders are not to let anyone in or out without an okay from

Mr. Pratt. Since Ms. Stenger works for him, I reckon that's pretty much the same thing. And I won't say a word to anyone, if that's what she wants."

The dilemma weighed heavily on Stenger's slim shoulders. Personal desire and professional responsibility visibly wrestled for control, and her conscience won. "All right. The two of you can go in. But don't say I didn't warn you it might not be a good idea."

HAL BROGNOLA HELD his breath as the person down the hall shuffled away. It hadn't spotted them, and entered a room at the far end of the corridor.

"We need a place to hide," he whispered to the terrified group.

"I know of one." Tim Wells hastened toward a door on their left. It was open a crack, and he pushed it wide with his shoe. "This is a rec room. There's a candy machine and a water cooler if anyone is hungry or thirsty."

Food and drink were the last things on Brognola's mind. Their survival was at stake, and they wouldn't last long if they barged into rooms as Wells had just done without verifying the rooms were empty first. Fortunately, luck was with them, and the room was empty. Brognola assisted Dr. Bellamy to a couch, then quickly shut the door and propped a chair against it.

Wells had made a beeline for the candy machine. "I'm hungry enough to eat my weight in candy bars," he announced. He fished in his pants pockets. "Damn. I forgot. They made me empty my pockets before the demonstration."

Brognola had a few quarters, which he shared. Then, squatting beside the couch, he gripped Bellamy's sleeve. "Doctor? Can you hear me? I need to know what we're dealing with, and how to stop them."

Chandler placed a palm on the scientist's forehead. "He's as cold as ice. Maybe we should let him rest a bit." He hobbled toward a chair.

The scientist's eyes fluttered open and he managed a weak

smile. "I'm okay," he rasped, red froth rimming his lower lip. "I must help while I still can."

Brognola pulled a handkerchief from his jacket pocket and wiped Bellamy's mouth. The froth was a bad sign. Severe lung damage, unless he was mistaken. "What are those things, Doctor? You started to tell me before, but we were interrupted."

"It's the extract," Bellamy said. "In its purest form it's the most powerful stimulant I've ever seen. Targets the adrenal glands. Causes the adrenal medulla to go crazy."

Bellamy had to stop. Froth lined his mouth again, and he needed to suck in air to breathe.

"The adrenal medulla?" Brognola was trying to remember basic physiology.

"It secretes epinephrine. Or adrenaline, as most call it. Increases the heart rate and blood flow. Boosts strength tremendously." Bellamy couldn't speak much louder than a whisper. "The simplest way I can describe the extract's effect is that it throws the human body into overdrive. So many hormones, the brain shuts down. Aggressive tendencies become dominant."

"Is there an antidote?" was Brognola's paramount question.

Bellamy frowned. "We never saw the need, never foresaw a breach of this magnitude." His eyelids drooped.

"Doctor?" Brognola shook Bellamy's arm. "You said something earlier about the condition being contagious?"

It took a lot out of him, but the scientist raised his head. "Not the condition. The extract. It can be absorbed through contact with contaminated sweat or saliva. It permeates the bloodstream in no time at all. Then the transformation takes place. Once triggered, there's no stopping it."

Brognola recalled how Tim Wells had returned to normal after a while. "But the effect wears off eventually, I take it?"

Sadness added mores lines to Dr. Bellamy's craggy face. "Not from the first-phase extract, no. The body burns itself out, like a battery that's used up all its energy. Eventually those affected will collapse and die."

"Even if they were to be hospitalized?" Brognola asked.

"Not even the best hospital in the world could help, no. It's irreversible. There is no cure. There is no hope." Bellamy clutched at Brognola's shirt. "That's why you must save as many as you can."

"I'll do what I can." Brognola had never felt more helpless.

Bellamy's grip tightened. "I created the extract. Blame for their deaths will fall on my head. I don't want that to be my legacy."

"You should lie still," Brognola advised.

Blood began trickling from a corner of Bellamy's mouth. He coughed a few times, groaned and sank back. "What difference does it make? I'm not long for this world anyway."

Lucy Reese leaned down. "Don't talk like that. My grandmother used to say that where there's life, there's hope."

"Optimism is one thing. Blind optimism is another." Dr. Bellamy tried to smile. "But I thank you for wanting to bolster my spirits." Another coughing fit struck him. It was so severe he doubled over and turned red. When it subsided he leaned back, exhausted, and closed his eyes. "I never thought I would end my days like this."

Brognola had one more crucial question he needed to ask before it was too late. "You must know this facility from bottom to top. Where's the best place for us to lay low until help arrives?"

The scientist could barely form the words. "Security station. Sublevel 6." His body went limp.

"Is he dead?" Reese asked.

Brognola felt for a pulse and found one, albeit faint and erratic. "Not yet. But he was right. He isn't long for this world."

Chandler had rolled up his left pant leg, exposing a nasty six-inch gash on his calf. "Neither are we if we think we can hide from those things. I vote we head for the surface."

"The elevators are out of commission," Brognola reminded his old friend. "The only other way is the stairwell. And we all heard what happened to Deever."

"If you want to stay down here cooling your heels, be my guest," Chandler said irritably. "But not me. I'm going topside. When the lockdown is lifted, I'll be the first one out."

Tim Wells had strayed to the door. "Hush up!" he whispered. "I think I hear something!"

Brognola crept over to listen for himself. The hallway was quiet. He figured Wells was jumpy. But the next moment, scratching on the other side proved him wrong. Someone was out there. Or would some*thing* be more appropriate?

The doorknob began to turn.

Wells was as white as a sheet. He backed up, but he didn't watch where he was going and collided with an end table. A lamp tottered, thumping the wall. Wells grabbed it before it could fall, but the harm had been done.

Whatever was out there threw itself against the door.

9

The keypad that allowed entry to the airlock was useless with the power out. Bolan and McCarter had to open the outer door manually. Bolan turned a metal spin wheel counterclockwise until the lock disengaged with a loud click, then McCarter gripped a long metal handle in both hands and shifted it to the left until the seal broke. There was a sibilant hiss, and the door swung outward a quarter of an inch.

"I should have my head examined," Gloria Stenger remarked. "Pratt will roast me alive if anything goes wrong."

"It's too late to change your mind," McCarter said.

Bolan tugged on the wheel, and the heavy door swung out. "Secure the airlock after us and no one will know," he said.

Ducking under the low lip, he stepped inside. "If you haven't heard from us by dawn, call that phone number I gave you."

The call would be routed to Barbara Price at Stony Man Farm.

"What do I tell the person who answers?" Stenger wanted to know.

"That we went in but never came out. They'll take it from there." Bolan stepped to one side to make room for the Briton. The airlock was big enough to accommodate only the two of them.

"Good luck," Stenger said as the young guardsman pushed the outer door shut.

"CHECK YOUR RESPIRATOR," Bolan said to McCarter once they were sealed in the airlock. He made sure his own was working properly. He turned to the spin wheel set into the inner door and spun it in the same counterclockwise direction. Again there was an audible click. Again air hissed, and the door swung slightly outward.

"Allow me." McCarter pushed it open wide enough for them to go through.

A tunnel sloped gradually down from the airlock, lit by emergency lights barely bright enough to pierce the gloom. It served as a conduit for a host of wires and pipes that fed into the underground complex.

"I've always fancied taking a stroll into the bowels of the earth," McCarter said. "I was a big fan of H. G. Wells and Jules Verne as a lad."

"That explains your fondness for *Scientific American*," Bolan said while taking the lead. The soft soles of their boots made no sound on the concrete floor. Were it not for the reedy rasp of their respirators, they might as well be ghosts. Which was how Bolan preferred it.

The soldier had to remind himself that this wasn't a typical op. They weren't penetrating enemy territory. Stealth wasn't essential. They could make as much noise as they pleased, and it wouldn't matter. Old habits, however, were hard to break, and he found himself moving as silently as he could.

As they made their way through the tunnel, Bolan used the time to mentally review the layout of the facility. There was no way of knowing which level Brognola was on, and it might be necessary to go from floor to floor until they found him. He estimated it shouldn't take more than a couple of hours, even if they had to poke their heads into each and every room.

"Did you hear something?" McCarter suddenly asked.

"What?" Bolan halted. He had been so absorbed in thought, he hadn't heard a thing.

McCarter was turning his head right and left. "I'm not sure. It sounded like a howl of some kind."

Bolan recalled the growls and snarls he had heard over the phone. "Could it have been a dog?" he asked.

"Possibly," McCarter said. "It was too faint to tell." He resumed walking. "Or maybe it was just my imagination."

Whatever it had been, it wasn't repeated.

In due course Bolan spied another airlock ahead of them. He gripped the wheel to spin it but stopped when McCarter peered through the rectangular window, and gestured.

"You better take a look at this."

A pair of legs jutted into view. Bolan craned his neck but couldn't see more. Whoever it was lay on the floor at the base of the door, and wasn't moving. He couldn't tell if the person was alive or dead. The most likely scenario was that the person had fallen victim to the biotoxin, which meant the airlock itself was contaminated.

"Do these suits come with a money-back guarantee?" McCarter made light of the risk they were about to take.

Bolan never hesitated. He went through the procedure of opening the door. At the sound of the prolonged hiss, he felt his gut involuntarily tighten. Exercising great care, he opened the portal enough to see the sprawled figure of a middle-aged man in a white lab coat. Blood framed the man's head like a scarlet halo.

"His throat has been ripped out," McCarter commented.

That it had. Bolan opened the door wider, stepped over the threshold and squatted. He had seen a lot of wounds in his time: gunshot wounds, knife wounds, wounds caused by wild animals. And he was willing to swear, then and there, that whatever ripped out the man's throat had done it with bared teeth.

McCarter bent. "I once saw a man who had been attacked by a husky he had been beating. The bloke's throat looked just like this. It had to be a dog."

"Then who closed and locked the airlock doors?" Bolan asked.

Whoever it was had left the victim there to rot. Bolan had a decision to make—whether to reach inside his biosuit for the Beretta, which might expose him to a biotoxin, or continue on unarmed. He stepped to the other door and aligned his faceplate with the window.

McCarter's shoulder brushed his. "That's peculiar. All the lights are out. Even the emergency lights."

A sense of unease gripped Bolan. They stepped back, and he slid his hand into an outer pocket for the flashlight he had brought in case of such a situation. He flipped the switch.

A shimmering beam illuminated the window. For a few seconds a face was caught in its glare. A face that seemed both human and yet somehow inhuman. A visage twisted into a brutish mask of sheer hatred. It was there, and in a flash it was gone.

"Bloody hell!" McCarter used his favorite epithet. "What was *that?*"

Springing to the door, Bolan directed the beam through the glass. It lit up a fifteen-to-twenty-foot section of corridor and washed over five or six prone forms. "More bodies," he announced, and moved so the Briton could see them, too. The nearest, a woman, looked as if she had been torn apart. Literally. Her clothes were in tatters, her stomach a scooped out bowl from which her intestines had oozed like so much slimy rope.

"No biotoxin did that," Bolan said.

"I know when to take a hint," McCarter responded. Unzipping his suit partway, he slid in his hand. When it came out again, he was holding a Glock Model 24, a compact version of the popular autopistol. He fed a round into the chamber.

Bolan switched the flashlight to his other hand and opened his suit in order to draw the Beretta 93-R from its shoulder rig.

"I knew I should have stuffed an MP-5 down my boxers," McCarter said with a lopsided grin.

"Open it up," Bolan directed. He stepped to the center of the airlock, his Beretta extended in one hand, the flashlight in the other.

The former SAS commando stayed well out of the potential line of fire. "Ready?" he said after spinning the wheel and gripping the edge of the door.

Bolan nodded, and tensed. His beam speared into a well of darkness, playing over the still forms on the floor and beyond. He was primed to shoot at the first hint of a threat but there was no sign of anyone, or anything, disposed to harm them.

Crouched by the door, his Glock held in a two-handed grip, McCarter said quietly, "This is your show. Lead the way. I'll cover your back." He produced his own flashlight.

Inching to the opening, Bolan looked right and left before committing himself. Even though the corridor appeared to be deserted, his combat-honed instincts were cautioning him to take it slow. He raised one leg over the lip, then the other. A few steps brought him to the dead woman.

"She's been chewed on!" McCarter whispered.

Bolan's cast-iron stomach served him in good stead. Teeth marks were all over the woman's throat and shoulders, and select areas lower down. Stepping over the remains, he skirted a man whose head was bent at an impossible angle to the body.

McCarter pressed his back to Bolan's and backstepped, matching strides. He flicked his flashlight into windows and doorways, his trigger finger curled around the Glock's trigger.

The security substation was midway down the corridor. Bolan noted that the door was wide open, the knob shattered. He eased on through, giving the space between the door and the wall a hasty scrutiny. Overturned chairs and a ream of scattered papers were evidence of a struggle. A few pencil-thin lights on a central console were aglow.

"What now, Mack?" the Briton asked.

"Block off the door as best you can. We don't want to end up like those people down the hall."

"I hear that," McCarter said, and took a step.

A shriek keened from somewhere below. Like the face in the airlock window, it was both human and inhuman, a cry unlike any Bolan ever heard. He swung toward the hall, the short hairs at his nape prickling.

"Between you and me, mate, we can't find the big guy and get out of this place fast enough," McCarter stated as he picked up a chair and sidestepped toward the door.

Bolan picked up another and swung it around so it faced the console. Taking a seat, he studied the controls. Compared to the high-tech equipment at Stony Man Farm, this was as basic as a transistor radio. It helped that every toggle switch, lever and button was labeled. One read Public Address System. He flicked it, then spoke into a microphone on a stand. "Testing," he said. "Testing, one, two, three."

A speaker high on the wall mocked him with its silence.

Bolan inspected the mike but found no On or Off switch. He saw a row of toggles marked Intercoms. Under the first was Lab 1, under the second Lab 2, and so on. According to the blueprints, the lower the number, the higher the floor. Flicking the first switch, Bolan said, "Is anyone there?"

The speaker crackled a few times but that was all.

Bolan tried other toggles. Nothing happened until he switched the toggle to Lab 14. Then, crystal clear, he heard soft whimpers and the sobs of a woman weeping.

"Can you hear me?" Bolan asked through the intercom.

The sounds abruptly stopped, and someone sniffled.

"I'm in the security post on Sublevel 6. If anyone is there, answer me." Bolan waited. When no one replied, he reached for the next toggle and was about to flick it when he realized the sniffling was becoming louder, as if the person were closer to the intercom at the other end. He tried one more time. "Is anyone there?"

"Yes!" came a frantic, whispered response. "I'm here! I'm here!" A choking sob escaped her.

"Stay calm," Bolan said, keeping his voice low.

"I'm trying," the woman cried, "but I'm so scared! Those things could be anywhere! I heard one right outside the door a while ago!"

"Things?" Bolan asked.

"Haven't you seen them? The ones who have changed? Who have transformed into hideous killers?" Her voice quaked and she sobbed anew.

"You haven't identified yourself," Bolan said to take her mind off her fear. "I'm Dr. Brown from the CDC. Who are you?"

"Carolyn Edmunds. I'm in Lab 14 on the floor right under you. I've barricaded the door but that won't keep those things out if they discover I'm here."

"Tell me more about them."

The woman took a few deep breaths to steady herself. "They attack and kill anyone they see. I saw two of them murder Billy Jones. He tried to fight back, but they were too strong. I can still hear his screams in my head. Those awful, terrible screams."

"Sit tight. My associate and I will be right down." Bolan sensed that McCarter had come up behind him. "One more thing. We were told some VIPs were visiting Spider Mountain today. You wouldn't happen to know which floor they were on when all this went down, would you?"

"I'm a lowly lab assistant," Edmunds said, "and information around here is on a need-to-know basis. But if Mr. Harkin was putting on another demonstration for bigwigs, it was probably on Sublevel 12. They do stuff like that down there all the time, but no one can get on that floor without a special clearance."

"Thank you. We should be there with you in a few minutes," Bolan said, hoping his soothing tone would help the woman stay calm.

"Dr. Brown?" A frantic note seeped back into her voice. "If you see one of those things, run! Or so help me God, you're as good as dead!" She started to cry again.

"OPEN UP, DAMN IT! It's me, Luther Harkin!"

Brognola ran to the door and yanked the chair away. The industrialist stumbled inside, then wheeled and immediately shut the door again, pressing his shoulder against it. He was ashen and trembling.

"One of those creatures almost caught me in the stairwell! I was lucky to get away alive!" Harkin was panting.

"You've led it to us?" Brognola almost punched him.

"How stupid do you think I am? It's still in the stairwell." Harkin steadied himself, and straightened. "There weren't any others in the hall just now. I did hear a lot of noise from over in Lab 24, though."

Lucy Reese stormed toward him. "You ran out on us, you miserable coward. We should throw you back out there and let them have you."

Harkin's arrogance reasserted itself. "I'd like to see you try. For your information, I was going for help. I thought if I could reach the security station on Sublevel 6, I might get through to my people up above."

"And pigs can fly," Reese said in disgust.

Brognola put a finger to his lips and his ear to the door. He thought he had heard a noise. But although he strained his ears for all they were worth, the corridor remained quiet. "I guess it was nothing," he told the others.

Tim Wells let out a long breath. "Don't scare us like that. I saw what those things can do when I was in that chair, and I don't want any part of them."

Harkin had been about to move toward the water cooler, but he stopped. "You were awake the whole time? Yet you didn't try to help? Young man, I have half a mind to fire you. I expect better of my employees."

Reese came to Wells's defense. "This from the coward who hid under the chairs when those monstrosities attacked us? If I make it out of this mess alive, I'm going to proclaim to the entire world what a craven waste of space you are."

"Do your worst," Harkin taunted. "My public-relations firm will turn you into a laughingstock. And a few words from me in the director's ear, and the CIA will give you your walking papers."

"You always were a backstabbing bastard," Reese snapped.

"While you, my dear, never quite grew up. To you, life is a fairy-tale realm where bad things shouldn't happen to good people. But that's not the real world. To survive, a person must be as ruthless as reality."

Brognola was tired of their bickering. "Let's talk about how we're going to survive. It would help if we had some idea of how many of your employees have been infected. Bellamy said all it takes is physical contact to spread the toxin from one person to another."

"Hal!" Bryce Chandler abruptly called out.

Brognola glanced toward his friend and saw Chandler gaping at the couch. Dr. Bellamy was sitting up. Blood still seeped from the scientist's mouth and his face was still deathly pale, but now his eyes blazed red and his lips were pulled back from his teeth.

The scientist was now infected.

10

The sleek Bell helicopter streaked in low over the Virginia terrain heading southeast. Its four occupants were decked out in black, including ski masks and gloves. Slung over their shoulders were MP-5s. Strapped around their waists were SIG-Sauer P-225s. Each man had a Ka-Bar fighting knife snug in a leg sheath. The pilot verified his heading and announced, "ETA five minutes, gentlemen."

"I still don't like this idea," Burt Anderson said. "We're bodyguards, not the CDC. This is way out of our league."

Tanner twisted toward the copilot seat. "So you keep saying. I think the rewards are worth the risk." He twisted even more to see the two men behind him. "Executive Protection was my brainchild, but we've all been involved since the beginning. So how about if we put it to a vote. Romero? Sax? What do you say? Do we pull Luther Harkin's fat out of the biopharm fire or do we tuck our tails between our legs and crawl back to D.C.?"

The taller of the pair grinned. His skin, what little of it was visible around the eye and mouth slits, was as dark as his ski mask. "When you put it that way, bro, I say we go for the gusto. No guts, no glory."

Anderson frowned. "Spoken like a true former SEAL. But you're not thinking this through, Sax."

The small, wiry man next to Sax had something to contribute. "*Lo siento,* amigo. But I go with them on this. Señor Harkin is *muy importante*. If we save a big man like him, other big men will hire us to protect them."

"Exactly, Romero," Sax declared. "We'll be rolling in greenbacks. And I didn't get into this business to end my days on skid row."

"It's obvious I've been wasting my breath." Anderson sighed. "Just so all of you know, I'm doing this under protest. Mark my words. No good will come of it."

Tanner was flying at near treetop level and had to gain altitude when an exceptionally tall maple loomed in their path. "Your protest has been noted," he said.

Tanner leveled off again. "Look, Burt. You've always been more cautious than the rest of us, and we appreciate you always looking out for our hides. But there comes a time when a man has to throw caution out the window and bite the bullet. Know what I mean?"

"Unfortunately, yeah." Anderson cradled his MP-5. "So I won't bring it up again. I only hope I don't have to say 'I told you so' later on."

Stars sparkled high above them. Otherwise, the night was as inky as the bottom of a well. Mountains reared on both sides, and they were all acutely aware that a single miscue on Tanner's part could splatter them all over creation.

Sax excitedly thumped the floor with a combat boot. "Man, it feels good to see some action again! Baby-sitting stuffed shirts pays great but bores me to tears."

"That makes two of us." Tanner veered westward, executing a wide loop that brought them up on the research facility from the opposite direction. He had done so for two reasons. First, to disguise their point of origin. Second, to take advantage of the terrain. A ten-mile-long valley bisected the range from the northwest, and for part of its length meandered along the western flank of Spider Mountain.

"What is that?" Romero pointed to the north. His eyes

were sharper than an eagle's, and he had spotted another aircraft when it was a mere speck on the horizon.

A few seconds later Sax said, "It looks like another copter."

"Take evasive action!" Anderson suggested.

Instead, Tanner held true to their course. "That's the last thing we want to do if they're Feds," he said. He gained altitude, to the normal ceiling for a chopper, and reduced airspeed. The other aircraft appeared to be on an intercept but then angled eastward, into the valley they were bound for.

"What do you make of it?" Romero wondered.

Tanner was more interested in the top of Spider Mountain. It was ablaze with light, including spotlights that crisscrossed the darkness from a dozen directions. "It's like a damn movie premiere."

"I'd take that as an omen," Anderson remarked. "We should call off this exercise in futility before it's too late."

"Like hell." Tanner copied the other helicopter's flight pattern. Elevation, airspeed, he shadowed them exactly. When the other copter angled up the forested slope toward the summit, so did he. When it slowed near the crest, so did he. But when it made for a landing site, he hovered, trying to wrap his mind around the scope of the scene below.

Anderson pointed. "Look at all those soldiers! I told you this was nuts. But would anyone listen to me? Nooooo!"

"It's lit up like Times Square," Sax commented. "No way in hell are we getting in there. Not unless we can turn invisible."

Romero shared their dismay. "*Madre de Dios*. I wouldn't even try. ¡*En absoluto!*" He blessed himself.

Tanner suddenly banked and circled to the north. "We can't let a little thing like a regiment of troops discourage us. There has to be a way in." He repeated it as much for his own benefit as for theirs. "There just has to be."

Sax jerked off his ski mask and ran a hand through his Afro. "We've been buds a long time, bro. When we got out of the Navy, I let you talk me into joining your protection gig. I'm always ready to back you one hundred percent." He gazed at the brightly lit compound, at the huge crowd at the main gate and at the guards posted at thirty-foot intervals around the chain-link fence. "But this time Burt is right. Luther Harkin is on his own. We'd best head home."

"A SEAL never gives up," Tanner said. "So what if it seems impossible? The only easy day was yesterday."

Sax jabbed a finger at him. "Don't you start reciting the SEAL motto to me, sucker. We're not SEALs anymore. Haven't been for seven years. And even when we were, we'd never take on our own boys in uniform. It just ain't done."

Tanner refused to buckle. "Who said anything about taking them on? Our objective is to slip in and out without a confrontation."

Anderson practically came out of his seat. "Do you need to have your eyes examined? There must be a hundred National Guardsmen down there. Granted, they're not Green Berets, but they're not idiots, either. And if they catch us in the act, I'm not lifting a finger against them."

"Me either, amigo," Romero said. "I have a cousin in the Guard. They serve our country just like everyone else."

Tanner slanted the Bell toward the research facility, taking care not to get too close. He scanned the fence, the grounds, the structures. Their best bet was to land as close to the main building as they dared, but the best spot was over a hundred yards from the entrance. The National Guard would stop them before they made it halfway. They would be carted off to jail. Harkin would be furious, and a lot of other clients might terminate their contracts to avoid being associated with EPI.

"What are we hanging around for?" Anderson asked. "It's not as if you can pull a miracle out of your mask."

Tanner's gaze had alighted on the milling throng of reporters and others outside the main gate, and he smiled. "That's where you're wrong, my friend. I have the answer to our little problem."

"There's nothing little about it." Anderson arched his back

to try to see what Tanner was looking at. "What's going on in that devious mind of yours?"

"We're heading back to D.C. To that storage unit we rent. There's some stuff in there we'll need. We can be back here by one a.m. By two we'll have Harkin out." Tanner laughed. "What could be easier?"

"Digging our own graves," Anderson said.

Stony Man Farm, Virginia

SO FAR, SO GOOD, Barbara Price thought, and leaned back in her chair. She removed the headset she had been wearing and wearily rubbed her eyes. It had been a long day and promised to be a longer night.

"I can spell you if you need a break," came a voice behind her.

Price hadn't heard Kurtzman wheel his chair into the Communications Room. She turned. "I'm fine, Aaron. Thanks."

"I brought you this." Kurtzman set a steaming mug of coffee in front of her. "Figured you could use some pick-me-up about now." He tapped the headset. "Anything new?"

"No word yet from Mack or David. To the best of our knowledge they made it inside. Jack saw them bluff their way through the front gate. Since then, zip." Price savored a sip of the delicious mocha, pleased surprise written on her face. "Keep spoiling me like this and it will go to my head," she said with a weary smile. "I was expecting your usual strong brew."

"Beware computer geeks bearing gifts." Kurtzman grinned. "I had someone bring it from the farmhouse."

Price chuckled. "You're hardly a geek. And if there's something on your mind, out with it. We've always been open with each other, haven't we?"

"Always." Kurtzman glanced at a pair of nearby techs,

then moved his wheelchair closer. "Even though we have the best of intentions, there is a very real possibility that the President won't like what we've done."

"I'm prepared to accept full responsibility. Any reprimands handed down will land in my lap. The rest of you needn't worry."

Kurtzman patted her hand. "That's just great, but do you honestly think we would let you be the fall girl? I've talked it over with the others and we all agree. We're in this together. If there's any flack, we all take the hit. Not just you."

Price was touched. "Thank them for me. It means a lot."

"I just pray everything works out. Losing Hal would be a calamity. Sure, the President could find a replacement. But it would never be the same. Hal is more than our boss. I consider him a close personal friend."

So did Price. He was always there for them, always willing to bend the rules a bit if that was what it took to get the job done and get their teams home safe and sound. Many a time Brognola had put his own neck in the administrative noose for their sakes. To lose him would be unthinkable.

A light began to blink. "Hold on a second," Price said. Slipping on the headset, Price pressed a button. Twice earlier she had monitored phone calls between Richard Pratt, the VDEM assistant director on-site, and the office of the Secretary of Public Safety.

Pratt was placing another call and Price wanted to monitor the whole conversation.

A woman answered, saying, "Operations Division."

Pratt asked to be patched through to Director Benjamin's office. He told her it was urgent.

"Benjamin here."

"It's Pratt, sir."

"What is it now, Richard? I just got off the phone with the secretary, and he's not entirely happy with how you've been handling this affair."

"I'm doing everything by the book, sir, as he'll see in my detailed report when this is over."

"I hope so, Richard, for your sake. Because all he's seen so far is your face plastered on every news channel. Media hogs have no place at the VDEM. We have a job, we do it. There's to be no grandstanding."

"I'm shocked, sir. Do you really think I would stoop that low?" Pratt waited for a reply. When none was forthcoming, he stated, "The reason I'm bothering you again has to do with the CDC."

"Is it another jurisdictional quibble? We've already established that you have oversight. But you're not to step on their toes, Richard. They have a job to do, and they do it extremely well."

"I think they're up to something, sir. It could be they're planning to undermine my authority somehow."

"Can you possibly be any more vague?" Director Benjamin sounded annoyed.

"They've sent two more people in without notifying me first," Pratt said. "Honchos from their home office. Clancy and Brown are their names. Clancy insisted on conducting an inspection so I was forced to agree."

"I fail to see the problem," Director Benjamin said gruffly. "In case I haven't made it clear, you are to give the CDC your full cooperation."

"You haven't heard the rest, sir. You see, I've been talking to the CDC decon team. They know nothing about Clancy and Brown."

Benjamin's impatience was growing. "So the CDC home office failed to notify them. So what?"

"It gets stranger, sir," Pratt said. "Clancy and Brown have disappeared."

"How's that again?"

"They've vanished, sir. I can't find them anywhere. I assigned Stenger to give them a tour, and she claims they told her they would rather be on their own. She acted nervous when I asked. I suspect she's in on it."

"In on what?' Benjamin paused. "You worry me, Richard. You truly do. The VDEM and the CDC have always worked hand in hand. You're supposed to coordinate our activities with theirs, not accuse them of some sort of juvenile conspiracy. The very idea is preposterous."

"But sir—" Pratt began.

"But nothing!" Benjamin was angry. "You will forget about Clancy and Brown. You will stop giving interviews to the media. You will concentrate on your job and *only* your job, and when this is over, we are going to sit down and have a long talk. Is that understood?"

Price listened until they hung up, then removed her headset and grinned

"Things are going well?" Kurtzman asked.

"They couldn't be better." The light blinked again and Price donned the headset. Richard Pratt was making another call. Or so she thought until she heard a woman's voice say to someone in the background, "Yes, I'll be right out. I have to call my sister and tell her I won't be able to meet her for breakfast as we'd planned." Only the woman wasn't calling her sister. The same secretary came on, and the woman also asked to speak to Director Benjamin.

"This is Gloria Stenger. I'm reporting as you requested, sir, but I have to say *I* don't like it."

"We need a set of reliable eyes and ears at the scene," Benjamin responded. "The VDEM has its image to maintain and, quite frankly, Pratt is doing us more harm than good with his theatrics. We don't need glory hounds like him making us look like fools."

"Surely you could keep tabs on him without my help?" Stenger asked.

"If we could, do you think I'd have contacted you after I saw him grinning into every TV camera shoved in his face? We have a high-profile crisis on our hands. If Pratt blows it, it will look bad for all of us." Benjamin paused to let that sink in. "Now report what you know, Gloria."

"The extra electricians have arrived. We hope to have the power up and running inside the hour."

"What about the telephones?" Benjamin asked.

"That may take a little longer. We thought we had a working line to the security office on Sublevel 6, but the phone at their end is off the hook and all we heard was a dog growling."

"Very well. Keep me posted. I want updates every hour."

Price thought Benjamin was about to hang up, but she was wrong. Every nerve in her body jangled when she heard his next comment.

"By the way, Pratt mentioned something about two men from the CDC. Clancy and Brown, I believe their names were. Where are they right at this moment?"

Stenger didn't answer.

"Gloria? Did you hear me?"

"I'd rather not say, sir."

"Why in the world not? Pratt suspects they're up to something fishy. From the way you're acting, I'd almost think he was right." Benjamin's tone hardened. "Refusal isn't an option. You will tell me, and you will tell me now."

Stenger's next words caused Price's stomach to churn.

"They went below, sir. They insisted it was necessary. But they should be safe. They were wearing biosuits, and they promised not to endanger anyone topside."

"They already have," Director Benjamin declared. "Something is wrong here, seriously wrong. I'm going to contact the CDC and find out who those two are. Then I'm flying out to take personal control of the situation. This incompetence has gone on long enough." The line at his end went dead.

Price stripped off her headset and swiveled her chair toward Kurtzman.

"What happened to your happy face?" he asked.

"We've got trouble, Bear. Big trouble."

11

Hal Brognola wasn't a Stony Man commando, but he had survived more than his share of danger. He had been shot at. He had nearly been blown to bits. He'd had cutthroats come at him with knives, chains and clubs. Not once had he flinched. Not once had he been completely overcome by the raw fear that spiked through him now.

Dr. Bellamy was slowly rising from the couch. Ghastly bloodshot eyes gazed at each person in the room in turn, as if he were trying to make up his mind which one to attack. From his open mouth trickled a steady stream of drool, and from deep in his chest came a rumbling growl more befitting a leopard than a human being.

Lucy Reese screamed.

Instantly Bellamy spun and lunged. Reese backpedaled, but she wasn't quite fast enough and Bellamy's hooked fingers snagged her jacket.

Brognola was compelled to act. He would be the first to admit he wasn't necessarily the bravest man in the world, but neither was he a rank coward. When someone was in peril, his natural impulse was to do what he could to help them. So without thinking, he hurled himself at the deranged scientist.

With a speed Brognola would never imagine Bellamy possessed, the doctor swung a bony fist in a vicious swipe. Brognola brought his arms up, blocking the blow, but it was still powerful enough to lift him clean off his feet and send him crashing against the wall.

Luther Harkin and Tim Wells were glued where they stood, but Bryce Chandler heaved out of his chair and moved to place himself between Bellamy and Reese. His leg hampered him, and before he could reach them, the scientist bent her back and opened his mouth wide to take a bite out of the woman's neck.

"No!" Reese cried.

Brognola cast wildly about for a weapon. Wells chose that moment to break his paralysis and leap onto Bellamy's back, locking his arms around the older man's. With frightening ease, Bellamy shook him off, then bent anew toward Reese.

By then Chandler had reached them. He punched Bellamy to try to distract him and was rewarded for his effort with a fist to the chest that knocked him back into the chair he had risen from. Chandler and the chair performed a somersault.

Reese was struggling to break free, but she was powerless against Bellamy's bioenhanced might. He pinned her against the wall, snarled hideously, and poised for a lethal bite.

It was now or never. Brognola launched himself into a driving run, pumping his legs as he had on the gridiron in his youth. He struck from the side to take Bellamy by surprise. His right shoulder slammed into the scientist's hip, momentum succeeding where his own strength wouldn't. Bellamy was flung a dozen feet, tripped over a table and toppled.

Seizing Reese by the arm, Brognola pushed her toward Wells. "Get out of here! Both of you!"

The door was already wide open; Luther Harkin had fled. Brognola turned to help Chandler out from under the chair, but his friend was already rising. So was Dr. Bellamy, who lurched toward them, his limbs jerking spasmodically.

"Fight the drug, Doctor!" Brognola urged. "Don't let it beat you!" He was wasting his breath.

Bellamy could no more resist the biotoxin's influence than anyone else had been able to. Sheer savagery filled his red-veined eyes. Pure, unreasoning animal ferocity. His pupils were dilated, his nostrils flared, his jaw muscles twitched nonstop. Sweat poured from every pore.

Brognola remembered Bellamy saying the toxin could be transmitted from person to person by a single drop of perspiration. When the scientist suddenly snatched at his hand, he darted aside to avoid contact.

Unnoticed by Bellamy, Chandler had picked up the chair, raised it over his head and was limping closer.

To keep the scientist occupied, Brognola retreated toward the doorway, shouting, "Come and get me! I'm the one you want!"

The scientist started forward, then stopped. Some sixth sense had warned him. He whirled just as Chandler swung the chair. It rocked Bellamy on his heels, the force sufficient to shatter the chair, but he didn't go down.

A rising sense of frustration seized Brognola. How could they hope to stop someone hopped up on a drug more potent than PCP? Someone with the adrenaline-fueled strength of five men and the lust for violence of a blood-crazed wolverine? Add to that the fact he wanted to avoid harming Bellamy if he could. After all, the scientist was a victim, not an enemy.

Chandler had no such compunctions. As Bellamy pivoted toward him, Chandler grabbed a broken length of chair leg and buried it in Bellamy's torso. The scientist arched his spine, then staggered a few feet, clawing at the crude spear. An angry hiss escaped him.

Favoring his wounded leg, Chandler pushed Brognola ahead of him to the door. "What are you waiting for? Haul butt while we can!" he urged.

Brognola didn't take his eyes off Bellamy until he was in the corridor. Wells and Reese were running toward the stairwell. Luther Harkin had already reached it and was impatiently urging them on. Brognola disliked being in the open, but the others weren't about to stop. He kept pace with Chandler, glancing into every door and window they passed.

"If we make it out alive," Chandler said through gritted teeth, "I'm going to have Harkin strung up by his thumbs and flayed alive. Legally speaking, of course."

"Of course," Brognola said. He'd have liked nothing better himself, but as far as he knew, Harkin hadn't broken any laws.

"Or maybe I'll have him injected with his own damn extract. Turnabout is fair play." Chandler continued griping.

Brognola wished his friend would shut up. He was trying to listen for more attackers. Where were the five from the VIP lounge? To say nothing of the scores of others that had to be roaming the facility?

Lucy Reese was flushed but unhurt, her fear back under control. "I'm sorry for how I behaved back there," she said as Brognola and Chandler caught up. "I don't know what came over me."

"I do," Chandler said. "It's called self-preservation. Don't blame yourself. We were all scared spitless." He stared at Luther Harkin. "Our host most of all."

Harkin had a ready retort. "If it's a sin to want to live, then I'm guilty. As far as I'm concerned, it's every man, or woman, for themselves."

"Quiet!" Brognola commanded. He thought he had heard a sound from the vicinity of Lab 24.

"Who died and put you in charge?" Harkin defied him.

Maybe it was the stress. Maybe it was the knowledge they were trapped like mice in a cage overrun by psychotic cats. Or maybe it was simply that Brognola had never liked Luther Harkin, and never would. Whatever the reason, something inside him snapped. Gripping the front of Harkin's shirt, he yanked the man up onto the tips of his toes. "I'll say this only once. To have any chance of making it out alive, we need to work together. So from now on, what I say goes. Is that understood?"

"Like hell!"

Brognola's knee arced upward. He let go of Harkin and the industrialist fell, hands over his crotch. "I trust I won't need to make my point again," he said.

Reese was grinning from ear to ear. "That was too sweet for words. Kick him a few more times for good measure."

Harkin glowered and opened his mouth to speak but changed his mind and closed it again.

As yet, there had been no activity down the hall. Brognola didn't know what to make of it, but he refused to tempt fate by going back there. "We're taking the stairs to the next floor. From here on we speak only in whispers," he said, doing the same. "Move quietly, and keep one eye cast behind you at all times." He laid hold of the door handle. "I'll check if the coast is clear."

One of the hinges creaked ever so slightly. Gloom blanketed the stairwell. Brognola couldn't see his hand at arm's length. He realized they would have to grope their way up. Easing pickings for the drug-crazed marauders.

"We need flashlights," he announced, and looked at Wells. "You work here. Do you know where we can find any?"

The young man shook his head. "Afraid not. I never had to use one."

"How about you, Harkin?" Brognola prodded.

"How the hell would I know?" The irate industrialist slowly unfurled. "I run a business empire. I don't keep track of every piddling stapler and paper clip."

Brognola checked the corridor again. There had to be a flashlight in one of the rooms. "Stay here. I'll have a look around."

"No reason you should go alone," Bryce said, limping next to him. "Two people can search faster than one."

"That leg of yours will slow you down too much if we run into trouble," Brognola stated. "I'd better do this alone."

Lucy Reese didn't agree. "My legs work just fine, and I can run like the wind when I'm scared enough. I'll help you," she volunteered.

Neither Harkin nor Wells offered to go along. Brognola hadn't expected Harkin to, but Wells disappointed him. He sidled along the right-hand wall with Reese at his elbow. They drew abreast of the recreation room and Brognola saw Dr. Bellamy on the floor, motionless.

Suddenly Reese gripped his wrist.

A thump from down the hall echoed. Brognola waited with bated breath for a predator to appear, but none did. He moved faster, to a closed door, and tried the knob. It was an office. "Dr. Kent" was engraved on a nameplate on the desk. Brognola checked the desk drawers while Lucy rummaged through a pair of file cabinets.

"Nothing," she whispered.

That left a closet in the corner. In it were a couple of lab coats, a sports jacket and a pair of shoes.

"One room down, twenty to go," Reese remarked.

Brognola slid into the hall, his back to the wall. He had gone only a few feet when he glanced at the stairwell and was shocked to discover Harkin, Wells and Chandler were gone. He went to turn back, but a gasp from Reese drew his attention to the doorway to Lab 24.

Someone had just shuffled out of it.

THE SILENCE was unnatural.

Bolan catfooted toward the stairwell, David McCarter watching his back.

More mutilated bodies impressed on him that more than one killer had to be involved. No one person could slay so many, not with bare hands and teeth. He wouldn't let down his guard for a split second.

The soldier stepped over a man whose head had been partially caved in, skirted another whose eyes had been gouged out and one ear half chewed.

"What the bloody hell is loose down here?" McCarter whispered. "A pack of cannibals?"

That was when a woman in a white smock emerged from a room less than a dozen feet away. Her back was to them, and she was apparently unaware they were there. Swaying as if drunk, she took several short steps, her arms flapping like featherless wings.

Bolan stopped and crouched, centering the Beretta between her shoulder blades.

He wasn't taking any chances. "Excuse me?" he called out. "We'd like to speak with you, if you don't mind."

In slow motion the woman turned. The front of her smock was stained crimson. Gore caked her chin. Bits of pink flesh clung to the teeth she bared as her obscenely drooling mouth yawned wide. Eyes as red as fireplace coals fixed on them like homing beacons.

"Damn!" McCarter breathed. "She's the one who's been doing the chewing!"

But was she the only one? Bolan wondered. The face in the airlock window had been a man's. "Hold it right there!" he ordered. "Put your hands in the air where we can see them."

The woman took an ungainly step, her body quivering as if she were on the verge of a fit. She growled, sweat glistening on her contorted face, and awkwardly raised a clawed right hand.

"Do we shoot her?" McCarter asked.

Bolan hesitated. On the list of things the elite commandos of Stony Man never did, gunning down innocent civilians ranked near the top. Containing collateral damage was a priority on every op. This one should be no different.

Suddenly the woman exploded into blurred motion. Bolan tried to sidestep while thrusting out his right foot to trip her, but she clamped her fingers onto his biosuit, shifted and slammed him into the wall.

McCarter was caught napping. The woman clutched his right wrist, pulled him toward her and punched him. She had to weigh sixty pounds less than he did yet her blow propelled him through the air as if he had been fired from a cannon. He hit the floor and skidded another nine or ten feet.

Bolan was in a quandary. His opponent wasn't a terrorist or a Mafia enforcer. She wasn't an enemy soldier or a fanatic. She was an ordinary American, a woman who had the misfortune to be in the wrong place at the wrong time. She might have a husband. She might have kids. Whatever had turned her into a drooling horror was to blame for her attempt on their lives, not the woman herself. He didn't want to hurt her if he could help it.

Another growl escaped from the woman's throat. She pounced with lightning speed, dug her fingers into Bolan's hood and wrenched. The hood shredded like so much paper. Bolan found himself virtually nose to nose with an aberration of nature.

The woman's red eyes bored into his. Roaring like a lioness going for the kill, she snapped her teeth at his jugular.

Bolan ducked under her arms and spun to the left. She closed in on him again, and he clubbed her across the temple with the Beretta. For most people that was usually enough to stop them cold, but the woman barely missed a beat. Screeching, she clawed at his eyes.

Bolan skipped back out of reach. But the woman was not to be denied. Her hands locked on to his wrists. Her mouth gaped wide. He tried to execute a hip toss, but he couldn't budge her. She, however, had no such problem, and hurled him into the wall so hard his ribs felt as they were caving in, and his knees buckled.

David McCarter rushed out of nowhere. He delivered a right cross that snapped her head back. He kicked her in the kneecap and followed through with a reverse leg sweep. It should have upended her onto her backside, but all it did was enrage her. Bending, she took hold of his left leg and began to twist it as if it were a stick she intended to break.

Bolan had restrained himself long enough. The woman was too strong, too unstoppable. Civilian or not, she was a potentially lethal threat and had to be neutralized or eliminated.

Bolan shot her in the leg. Most people would have collapsed in agony. She merely snarled and swung toward him. He shot her again, in the shoulder this time, seeking to stop her rather than slay her. But while the slug whipped her halfway around, it didn't put her down.

Screeching like an alley cat, the woman leaped, her hands and teeth slashing at Bolan's throat.

"I'm sorry," he said, and shot her between the eyes.

For over a minute the body convulsed and flopped wildly about. McCarter stared in undisguised revulsion. "How could she do that? It was like fighting the bloody Bride of Frankenstein."

"What I want to know," Bolan said, "is how many more are there like her running around down here?"

"Do you think this is why the lockdown was imposed?" McCarter gazed at the shredded hood. "What if it's something in the air?"

Bolan touched his gloved left hand to his unprotected face. "Then I might already be infected," he said.

"I'm probably wrong," McCarter said quickly. "What say we push on before another of these beauties tries to turn us into sushi?"

"I'll go first," Bolan said. If he truly had been infected, it didn't matter. If he wasn't, then the air was okay to breathe, in which case it still didn't matter.

"What if..." McCarter said, but he couldn't continue.

"What if Brognola has become one of those things?" Bolan voiced the unthinkable. "We'll do our best to take him alive. But if he's anywhere near as strong and wild as she was, kid gloves aren't an option."

"That's cold," McCarter said.

"Better cold than dead."

Bolan peered into a room on their left. It was like looking into a black hole. "Watch this one after we go by."

"I'm watching every doorway," McCarter assured him.

From somewhere behind them a high-pitched scream rent the stillness. They spun, their flashlights slicing the dark veil. But all that moved in their twin beams were dust particles.

Bolan tapped the Briton on the shoulder and moved on. He didn't want to keep Carolyn Edmunds waiting any longer than necessary. She had to be beside herself with terror.

"Someone is shadowing us," McCarter whispered.

Not one but two vague shapes had materialized at the limit of McCarter's flashlight beam. They stood there, watching, their eyes vivid red against the backdrop of solid black.

Bolan wondered why they were holding back. He faced forward, anxious to reach the stairs, but halted as if he had smacked into a wall. Two more killing machines blocked the way.

12

"They're popping up out of the woodwork!" David McCarter declared, covering the pair behind them. "How can we reach the stairs without killing more of these poor sods?"

Bolan wanted to avoid another clash, but he wasn't given the choice. The two twitching forms in front of him uttered feral roars and bounded to the attack. Whatever was pumping through their veins gave them the speed of cheetahs. In the time it took Bolan to blink, they covered half the distance. As with the woman before them, their lips were drawn back, their fingers hooked like claws.

Under ordinary circumstances Bolan would have gunned them down. But these were not ordinary enemies. He sought to spare their lives by shooting each in the leg. It slowed them, it broke their strides, but it didn't deter them. To the contrary. Wounding them fed their frenzy. They howled all the louder and kept coming.

Simultaneously, the pair at the rear closed in. McCarter sighted down the Glock but delayed squeezing the trigger until they were in what he liked to think of as his personal never-miss zone. He was good with a pistol—maybe not quite as good as Bolan—but good enough that he was rated at one-hundred-percent accurate with targets out to twenty yards. So he let the pair get within the twenty-yard zone, then sent a slug through each of their craniums.

Bolan went for the head, too, now that wounding hadn't

worked. He felt no satisfaction in taking them down. It was like shooting diseased livestock. Something that had to be done but left a bitter taste afterward. He killed the first one swiftly enough, then sent a round into the forehead of the second. That should have done the trick. A 9 mm Parabellum mangler to the brain could stop almost anything. Incredibly, the thing kept coming, its teeth gnashing together, its fingers clenching spasmodically. Bolan shot it again, and a third time, before the abomination pitched to the floor, almost at his very feet.

"You let that one get a little close, didn't you?" McCarter said.

"I don't like killing innocent civilians," Bolan responded.

"My rule of thumb is that when someone tries to off me, I don't care if it's a cartel triggerman or the bloody Pope. I repay the favor. I'll live longer that way."

The stairwell door was ajar. Using his toe, Bolan eased the door all the way open. He looked up, then down, and saw a body halfway up the next flight, an older man missing the lower half of his face. He checked behind the door before moving to the rail.

McCarter backed through the doorway, his Glock trained on the hall. "Clear back here. But I thought I heard a growl a moment ago."

Bolan started down, step by cautious step. Now was not the time for reckless haste.

The Briton fell in behind him. "Still clear," he whispered.

"We're not alone." Bolan could feel it in his bones. Unseen eyes were on them. Lurkers in the dark were waiting for the right moment to strike. Which told him the afflicted workers had to possess a rudimentary cunning, thereby making them doubly dangerous.

"Saw something," McCarter said, and stopped.

So did Bolan. "What?"

"I'm not sure. A face, an arm, two flights up."

"They're stalking us." Bolan resumed the descent.

"What I wouldn't give right about now for a couple of hand grenades or an M-60," McCarter said.

The next landing was empty, the door closed. Bolan cracked it open and swept the corridor from side to side with his flashlight. Several more bodies added to the toll. A window on the right had been shattered, a door on the left hung by one hinge. "They've been here. Or still are."

"Refresh my memory. Who was it said we could pack light on the hardware? I brought only one spare mag along."

"How were we to know?" Bolan said. But the Briton had a worrisome point. He had two extra magazines, himself. If there were a lot of red-eyed lunatics running around, and the evidence indicated there were, it spelled trouble when their ammo ran out.

A wavering howl keened out of the bowels of the building, answered by another on a floor somewhere above.

In all his missions Bolan had never encountered anything like this. People transformed into murderous psychopaths. He would love to know what caused it, and tried not to think about the loss of his hood. "David?"

"Right behind you, mate. And hoping to hell I don't end my days as a zombie buffet."

Bolan gave it to him straight. "If I start to act strange, do what you have to. Take my pistol, find Hal and get him out."

"Strange? What are you talking—" McCarter stopped. "Oh. How about if we cross that bridge when we come to it? In the SAS we never left one of our own behind. I'd hate to break with tradition."

"It's not debatable. Our objective is to rescue Hal. Whether we like it or not, you and I are expendable," Bolan said.

"You sure know how to boost a bloke's confidence. If we make it out alive, you really should take up psychiatry," McCarter replied.

Lab14 was stenciled on a door on the left in bold letters. Bolan knocked but received no answer. "Ms. Edmunds? It's Dr. Brown from the CDC."

The door swung inward and a distraught young woman with disheveled sandy hair beamed for joy. "At last! I was beginning to think you wouldn't make it." She saw the Beretta. "Wait a minute. Since when do CDC field operatives carry side arms?" She looked terrified again.

"We're with the enforcement branch of the Biohazard Division," McCarter improvised. "You would be surprised at the number of genetically altered animals we've had to put down after experiments went awry."

"There aren't any animals down here," Edmunds said.

"No. Just a bunch of people acting like animals," McCarter countered. "Frankly, we didn't expect this. But our motto is to always be prepared."

"I thought that was the Boy Scout motto," she said.

McCarter never batted an eye. "Who do you think we swiped it from?"

Bolan backed into the lab. "Is there anything here that will help us against those things?"

"Help you how? As an antidote?" Carolyn Edmunds shook her head. "I don't know what changed them in the first place. It must have something to do with the special projects on the bottom level. That's where most of the ultra-secret experiments are conducted." She started to move past them. "Now get me out of here, if you please, and I'll be eternally grateful."

"We can't." Bolan wasn't leaving without Brognola. "A lockdown has been imposed."

Edmunds was flabbergasted. "That's insane! There won't be anyone left if they wait too long to lift it. They should quarantine us topside." Desperation seized her, and she grabbed hold of McCarter. "Please! You've got to do something!"

"We'll protect you as best we can," the Briton offered. "That's all we can do for the moment."

Bolan fully expected her to succumb to panic. Her eyes widened and she pushed McCarter away from her, then stood like a terrified fawn about to bolt. He nipped her flight in the bud by saying, "It's a long way to the lobby. You'll be on your own, with those crazies everywhere."

"But I want out!" Edmunds screamed. Overcome by the intensity of her emotions, she moaned and buckled at the waist.

"I'll be damned. She's fainted!" McCarter exclaimed, and caught her before she hit the tiles. Hoisting her into his arms, he deposited her on a couch. Her dress had hiked above her knees and he smoothed it back down again.

"I had no idea you were such a gentleman," Bolan remarked as he raked the corridor with his flashlight. As near as he could tell it was still empty.

"It's all that rot we're fed as kids," McCarter said. "Sir Galahad and King Arthur. Knights in shining armor rescuing fair damsels in distress." McCarter reached up and gripped his biohood. "It never entirely wears off."

"What are you doing?" Bolan asked a split second too late.

McCarter had removed the hood and was sniffing the air, testing it. "The bloody thing is a royal pain in the arse. I couldn't see to either side, and I was sweating like a hog in a slaughterhouse."

"But the risk," Bolan warned.

"You've had yours off a while, and you haven't dropped dead yet or turned into a zombie." McCarter set the hood on a table. "I have a feeling we'll run into more of those things before we find Hal. A lot more. And I don't want anything slowing me down." He reached for the biosuit's zipper. "Fact is, I'd just as soon take off the whole outfit."

"No." Bolan's suit hampered him, too, but it was the price they paid for extra protection. "It's bad enough you took off the hood. At least one of us has to make it to Hal."

"Implying that without your hood, you might not?" McCarter's grin was grim. "I've got news for you, mate. In the SAS it was all for one and one for all. We trained and worked as a unit. Same as Phoenix Force. What was good for one was good for everyone. That hasn't rubbed off just because I'm on a solo mission with you."

Bolan let the issue drop. I was pointless to argue. "I'll stand guard," he said. "Revive her so we can keep looking."

McCarter walked to a sink. In a cabinet beside it were beakers, test tubes and other containers, including a few glasses. He selected one, filled it and sat on the edge of the couch. Sliding a hand under the woman's head, he gently cradled her, then slowly tilted the glass so the water trickled between her parted lips.

Edmunds coughed several times, and her eyes shot open. She looked around in wild fear, then focused on the face above hers. "Oh. It's you. You're a lot more handsome without that hood on." She smiled up at McCarter.

"Thanks. And may I compliment you on your impeccable taste?" Grinning, McCarter helped her to sit up and gave her the glass. "Drink some more of this. Then we'll be on our way."

"Why go anywhere when we're safe here?"

"We're searching for some people who were caught down here when all hell broke loose. We've got to push on until we find them."

"Those VIPs Dr. Brown told me about?" Edmunds sipped some water. "How many are there?"

"We're not sure." McCarter removed the magazine from his Glock to verify the number of rounds he had left.

"Why are you frowning?" Edmunds asked.

"A man like me doesn't like to be caught short. Weapons are my stock-in-trade, you might say, and to leave home without them is like a doctor leaving home without his black bag."

"But I thought you are a doctor? With the CDC?"

McCarter could ooze charm with the best of them when he wanted. "Which was why I made the analogy. Or would it have made more sense if I compared it to a mechanic leaving home without his tools?"

Edmunds placed her hand on his right glove. "You sure

have a way with words. And I love your accent. What was it like being raised in the South? I've heard the countryside is beautiful."

Bolan cleared his throat. "If you're up to it, Ms. Edmunds, we have to get going. Save the chitchat for later."

"Sorry. I didn't mean to be nosy." She set down the glass and offered her arm so McCarter could assist her to her feet. "Is Dr. Brown always so devoted to his work?"

"He's the most dedicated man I know," McCarter said.

The corridor was still deserted except for the bodies, but Bolan couldn't shake the persistent feeling they were being watched every step of the way. He positioned Edmunds between McCarter and himself, saying to her, "Whatever you do, whatever happens, don't stray from our side."

Edmunds clutched the Briton's shoulder as if it were a lifeline. "Don't worry on that score, Dr. Brown. I don't intend to be ripped to pieces like some of the others have been."

The research facility was heavy with an ominous silence. The fierce cries had died. The wails and shrieks had faded.

Bolan advanced with the wariness of a seasoned soldier. His flashlight pierced the murky darkness that threatened to close around them like a glove once his battery ran low. Again he pried open the stairwell door. Furtive rustling greeted him, but whether from above or below he couldn't say. He crept to the rail. Was it his imagination, or did a pale face peer up at him for the span of a heartbeat, then melt into the shadows?

"I've never been so scared in my life," Edmunds whispered.

"Makes two of us," McCarter said. "Now bite that pretty tongue. Not a peep, you hear? We can't count on our eyes in this soup. Our ears have to take up the slack."

Which was easier said than done, Bolan mused, when every sound was reflected and distorted, making it nearly impossible to gauge direction and distance. It was like being in a carnival funhouse where nothing was as it seemed and a new monster lurked behind every door.

A growl wafted from above, followed by the patter of shoes on the metal stairs.

"They're pacing us," McCarter reported. "Can't tell how many yet."

Oddly, Bolan detected no crazies below. But there had to be some down there. He wondered if they were coordinating their efforts in some unfathomable manner, if maybe he and the others were being drawn into a trap. Was it possible the red-eyed horrors possessed more guile than he gave them credit for?

"I can try to pick a few off and lower the odds," McCarter proposed. He was leaning out over the rail, his flashlight pointed straight up.

"Save your ammo," Bolan directed. They would need every round they had when the big rush came. As he was sure it would. He slowed as another landing unfolded before them.

In the center lay another victim, or what little was left of him. Both arms had been torn from their sockets, his chest was a mass of shattered ribs and his neck was attached by a sliver of flesh.

"Dear God!" Edmunds gave a sharp intake of breath.

"Don't look," Bolan said, stepping in front of her.

She placed her hands on the rail and closed her eyes. "I don't know how much more of this I can handle."

Bolan felt sorry for her but she was delaying them. and every second counted. "Try not to think of it and keep moving."

Edmunds gave the corpse a wide berth and inadvertently stepped from between them.

"That's a no-no, remember?" McCarter said, pulling her back again. "We're your insulation, you might say, but we can't protect you if you don't listen to what we tell you."

"Sorry. I just wasn't thinking."

"I have the same habit." McCarter grinned, and would have said more except Bolan signaled for silence.

Loud footsteps rang on the stairs below. The crazies had ended their game of cat and mouse and were attacking in earnest.

13

The Executioner hurried to the end of the landing and played his flashlight over the next flight of steps. Crouching, he aimed at the point where the beam met the darkness. The pounding became louder. He had expected that, but not what came next.

"Hurry up, damn you!" a gruff voice commanded. "Can't you see that light? There must be others who haven't been infected."

"I'm trying, sir. I truly am. But I'm worn out from that demonstration you had me give."

"You're young. You'll get over it. Quit being a wimp and catch up," the first voice ordered.

Bolan had seen file photos of Luther Harkin, and he recognized the industrialist immediately. But there was also a much younger man, stripped to the waist, who plodded upward as if on his last legs.

"Hold it right there," Bolan commanded.

Harkin squinted up into the glare. He had on an expensive three-piece suit and a tie, and gave the impression he just stepped from a board meeting. But the sweat bathing his face and his shortness of breath belied it. "Who do you think you are, mister, giving me orders?"

Edmunds forgot herself and darted to the rail. "These men are doctors from the CDC, Mr. Harkin! They're here to help us," she said.

"Edmunds? Is that you?" Harkin stomped up the steps like an irate bull. "Explain to these fools who I am. Saving me has just become their highest priority. I demand they take me to the surface right this instant."

McCarter took his eyes off the stairwell above long enough to remark, "I've always wanted to meet the Almighty. But I thought he would be a bit more impressive."

Harkin wasn't the least bit amused. "What the hell is that crack supposed to mean? I'll report you to your superiors if you don't show more respect."

Bolan was watching the younger man climb painfully toward them. The man was about done in. "Where are the VIPs who were invited to the demonstration you mentioned?" he asked him.

"Most of them are dead," the young man stated. "And the few who are left soon will be, if they're not already."

"I don't like the sound of that," McCarter commented.

Neither did Bolan. He was about to help the younger man up the last few steps when more footfalls resounded below. Plodding, uneven steps, like those of the crazies. The young man heard, too, and scurried onto the landing with newfound vigor.

"They're after us, Mr. Harkin!"

"Keep your head, you spineless jellyfish."

Harkin motioned at Bolan. "Shoot it the moment it appears. Don't miss, either. All our lives are at stake."

"Get behind me and keep your mouth shut," Bolan replied. He had rarely met anyone he had immediately disliked so intensely. Harkin was one of those people who rubbed everyone the wrong way. The kind who felt it was their natural right to lord it over others. The kind who deserved a solid belt in the mouth.

"How dare you address me in that tone!" Harkin bristled. "I wield considerable influence, in case you haven't heard. You don't want me for an enemy. I can make your life miserable."

Bolan concentrated on the footsteps. The thing was close, maybe the next flight down. He shifted the flashlight and glimpsed a vague shape, bent over, one hand gripping the rail for support.

"Didn't you hear me?" Luther Harkin demanded. "You're just about the rudest doctor I've ever met."

Bolan locked eyes with Harkin. "Not another word out of you until I say you can talk." He took aim with the Beretta. The shuffling figure below was almost visible. Another couple of steps, and the head rose into plain sight. The eyes weren't red; the face was calm but resolute.

"That's no zombie," McCarter said.

The man heard. "Don't shoot! I'm Bryce Chandler of the NSA." His left leg was next to useless, and he had to drag it after him. Sweat dripping from his chin, he reached the landing and sank down with a groan.

Although Harkin Industries had kept the list of VIPs a secret, Price and Kurtzman had learned Chandler was one of them. And that the NSA operative had a history with Brognola.

"We have a mutual friend," Bolan said.

"We do?" Chandler was rolling up his left pant leg. The leg itself was badly swollen and discolored.

"Hal Brognola," Bolan said. "Do you know where he is?"

"The last I saw of Hal, he went to look for a flashlight." Chandler glared at Luther Harkin. "Then this miserable son of a bitch and Wells ran out on us. I went after them, yelled for them to stop, but they just kept climbing."

"So did you, I see," Harkin said sarcastically. "This is a case of the pot calling the kettle black."

"Like hell!" Chandler snapped.

"I'd like to hear the whole story," Bolan urged him.

"There's not much more to tell," Chandler said. "We were on the bottom level. After Harkin deserted us, I went to find Hal and the woman he's with, Lucy Reese. But a berserker was coming toward the stairwell so I climbed for dear life. And here I am." He touched his left leg and had to grit his teeth against the agony.

"A berserker?" McCarter repeated. "Is that what you call them? We've named them crazies."

"Call them whatever you want," Chandler said, mopping his forehead. "The important thing is not to let them touch you. The biotoxin is spread through physical contact. Once you get the stuff in your system, there's nothing anyone can do."

"So you have no idea what happened to Hal and Lucy Reese?" Bolan asked.

"No. I didn't dare stick around. If that berserker had seen me, I'd have been done for. They're inhumanly strong and fast," Chandler said apologetically.

"We know," McCarter said. "Any idea how many there are?"

Luther Harkin answered. "There could be fifty. There could be a hundred. Which is why we can't stand around babbling. We must reach the surface without delay."

"I agree," Tim Wells said. "I don't relish the thought of being turned into one of those zombies."

Bolan was thinking of what it had to be like for Brognola, trapped somewhere down below with crazies all over the place. "You two can go on if you want. But we're not leaving without Brognola and the other woman."

Harkin swore under his breath. "Forget your futile heroics. The deeper you descend, the less the chance of making it out alive. Escort us topside and I promise that as soon as it's practical, I'll send a fully equipped team down after them."

"That could be hours from now," Bolan said. Hours Brognola didn't have.

"What I'd like to know," McCarter interjected, "is how this whole marvelous mess started."

"Who knows?" Harkin shrugged. "Maybe when the lights went out, a lab assistant spilled some of the extract on his skin. Or dropped a vial. Or maybe some vapors seeped into the ventilation system." He scratched his chin. "Given how rapidly it spread, that would be my guess."

"But if the ventilation system was responsible," Chandler said, "why were some people affected and others weren't?"

"You're asking me? I'm not a scientist," Harkin scoffed. "Maybe some of the grates were open and others weren't. Maybe the vapor dispersed unevenly." He moved to the next flight and placed his foot on the first step. "Now's not the time to discuss this. I'm getting out while I still can."

A growl froze him in his place.

Bolan spun. A squat form was crouched at the next turn, ready to pounce. McCarter's flashlight beam washed over it, and the thing flattened and skittered back out of sight like some oversized lizard.

"Why didn't it attack?" Bryce Chandler asked.

Harkin had backed up several strides, his cockiness shaken. "Would you rather it had? What kind of simpleton are you?"

"The berserkers usually attack on sight," Chandler said. "They're mindless, raging brutes. Or so we've assumed. But what if we're wrong? What if a spark of intellect remains?"

Bolan had had the same idea. It did not bode well.

"So what?" Harkin rejoined. "A moron with a shred of intellect is still basically a moron. We'll put your idea to the test one day under laboratory conditions. All that's important at the moment is my welfare."

Carolyn Edmunds had absorbed the conversation in thoughtful silence until now. "Mr. Harkin, I hope you'll forgive me for saying this, but you're the most self-absorbed person I've ever met. All you care about is yourself."

"Forgiveness is for saints and morons." Harkin sniffed. "Of which I am neither."

Bolan ignored them and pondered the problem at hand. Namely, rescuing Brognola. It would take McCarter and him to do the job right, but he was loathe to leave Bryce Chandler alone and unprotected. He knelt beside him. "How are you holding up?"

"My leg is throbbing to beat the band, but I can stand if I have to." Chandler's eyes narrowed. "Why?"

"We can't wait any longer. We have to find Hal. I'd like for you to come with us."

Chandler shook his head. "I'd only slow you down. You can't baby-sit me and watch your backs at the same time."

McCarter came over. "How about if we compromise?" he suggested to Bolan, and nodded at the stairwell door. "We'll find a secure room for him to lie low in until we've extracted Hal and the woman, then collect him on the way out." A sharp cry drew his gaze upward. "And we'd best be right quick about it."

The NSA man glanced from Bolan to McCarter and back again. "You two work for the CDC, eh?" He smiled slyly. "I was born yesterday, too."

Harkin was angrily rapping a hand on the rail. "What are you three whispering about?" he demanded to know.

From below came a metallic clang and the titter of insane laughter.

Bolan slid an arm under Chandler's. "Let's find you that room."

McCarter was all set to do the same on the other side but Edmunds beat him to it, saying, "One of you should have your hands free in case we're attacked."

Slowly opening the door, Bolan confirmed the corridor was empty before venturing into it.

"Shouldn't we go with them?" Tim Wells asked his employer.

"You'll stick with me, and that's an order," Harkin haughtily replied. "Unless you plan to look for a new job tomorrow."

"But they have flashlights and we don't."

Wells said more, but Bolan didn't hear what it was. The door closed, muffling the young man's voice. McCarter slipped in front, taking point.

The absence of bodies was encouraging. Nor did Bolan see any broken windows or smashed doors.

"Known Hal long, have you?" Chandler unexpectedly asked.

Bolan didn't insult the man by lying. "Long enough that I'd hate for anything to happen to him. He's one of the good guys."

"One of the all too few," Chandler agreed. "When this is over, we should all get together for a drink and talk tradecraft."

"I doubt we'll ever see each other again," Bolan said. He wasn't fooled. Chandler's curiosity had been piqued, and he was fishing for information. "In my line of work I'm never in one place very long," he added in a suitably vague explanation.

Edmunds couldn't help but overhear, and misconstrue. "It must be rough, having to travel all over the country dealing with situations like this. The stress alone would be more than I could bear."

McCarter motioned for them to stop. He was staring at a window on the left. "Thought I saw something move," he whispered, and padded forward to investigate.

"I've never felt so scared in my life," Edmunds softly mentioned. "It's like waiting for the guillotine to drop."

Firming his grip on the Beretta, Bolan tensed as McCarter gingerly tested a doorknob. The door swung silently open and the commando slipped inside. The seconds ticked by weighted by millstones, with Bolan on edge. Just when he was about to have Chandler and Edmunds wait while he checked on the Briton, McCarter's muscular frame filled the doorway, and he beckoned.

"This should do nicely," McCarter said.

Chandler winced as Bolan and Edmunds lowered him into a chair in a plush office. "What I wouldn't give for some painkillers or an ice machine."

"There's one in the lounge on the floor above us," Edmunds told them. "Which doesn't do us much good, I'm afraid."

Bolan snatched up the phone on the desk, but it was dead. While McCarter stood guard at the door, Bolan rummaged through a desk. All he found was a small tin of aspirin. Only four tablets were left. "Will these do?" he asked Chandler.

"They're better than nothing." Chandler upended all four into his palm and popped them into his mouth.

"We'll lock the door behind us," Bolan said. "Don't make any noise, and you should be fine until we return."

"He's not staying alone," Edmunds declared. "It wouldn't be right, someone in his condition." She stood beside the chair. "I'll watch over him."

The NSA man squeezed her hand. "I appreciate the sentiment, young lady, but you should stick with these gentlemen. They can protect you. I can't."

"Who says the age of chivalry is dead?" Edmunds bantered, and gestured at the Stony Man duo. "Go on. Get out of here before some of those things show up. We can manage on our own."

On the one hand, Bolan was glad she wanted to stay. He and McCarter would make a lot better time, and wouldn't have the added burden of having to protect her. On the other hand, it went against all he was and all he believed in to leave them there alone, defenseless. Especially her.

"You know, I've been thinking," McCarter began.

Exactly what the Briton had on his mind was eclipsed by a hideous shriek from the stairwell. Not the demented cry of a berserker, but a full-throated scream of pure and total torment. Of someone in unendurable agony. It became a high-pitched wail that seemed to go on forever, then faded like a ghost in the wind.

"That was Tim Wells," Bryce Chandler said.

Bolan thought so, too.

McCarter suddenly pivoted. "You'd best give a listen out here, Dr. Brown. I don't like the sound of this."

The soldier moved to the doorway. Someone—a lot of someones—was raising more racket than a frenzied crowd at a football stadium. Drumming feet, fierce howls and wolfish yips coalesced into a fearsome chorus. As he looked on, the stairwell door was shoved wide and down the corridor barreled Luther Harkin, fleeing as if the hounds of Hades were after him. And indeed, they were. For out of the stairwell poured berserker after berserker, snapping and grinding their teeth in abandon.

"Save me!" Harkin bawled.

McCarter extended his Glock. "The bloody jackass," he spit, and fired. A crazy about to grab the industrialist toppled. Those behind it tried to stop or leap over the body, but their own momentum and that of the berserkers on their heels knocked five or six of them to the floor and a pileup resulted.

It bought Luther Harkin the precious seconds he needed to reach the office. "Thank God I've found you! They've killed Wells," he cried.

"Too bad they didn't kill you!" McCarter said in disgust, and shot another attacker smack between the eyes.

Bolan moved aside so the industrialist could scurry past him. Then, stepping in front of the Briton, he assumed a combat crouch, the Beretta in a two-handed grip. He had the most ammo. It was only fair he bear the brunt of the attack. He fired into the writhing mass, aiming for heads. Three, four, five times he squeezed the trigger, and at each retort, a berserker sprawled flat.

It wasn't enough.

The rest scrambled over the bodies, pushing and shoving one another in their eagerness to tear into living flesh.

"Back inside!" McCarter yelled.

The urging wasn't needed. Bolan couldn't hope to stop that many with just the Beretta. Not endowed as they were with superhuman strength and ferocity. He backed into the office, and McCarter slammed the door and locked it.

Moments later fists hammered heavily on the other side.

"Whatever you do, don't let them in!" Luther Harkin whined. He was cowering behind a file cabinet.

Red-eyed apparitions filled the window, their teeth bared, their faces contorted. Fingers hooked like talons rasped on the glass.

"We're trapped!" Edmunds cried. "What do we do? How can we keep them from getting in?"

Bolan frowned. The answer to that was simple—they couldn't.

14

Like a dragonfly whisking over a pond, the Bell helicopter flew in low from the east. In defiance of the law, its running lights were off. Invisible in the darkness, it skimmed the tree-tops on a course that would soon bring it to the top of the next mountain. Inside, four figures clad in skintight blacksuits were as still as statues until Tanner announced, "This is it, boys. Remember the drill we've worked out, and it'll be as easy as pie."

"You hope," Burt Anderson amended.

The Spider Mountain Research Facility hove into sight. Spotlights continued to illuminate the site, including the crowd at the main gate. The buildings, though, were still dark.

"Good," Tanner declared. "Everything is just as we want it." In a few seconds the copter was clear of the trees and he dipped almost to ground level, angling the Bell toward the makeshift airfield. He was relying on the aircraft already parked there to conceal their approach.

Romero crossed himself. "Madonna preserve us." He picked up the gas mask in his lap. "Here goes nothing."

Sax patted a spare magazine in a pouch on the web belt at his waist. "I'm locked and loaded and primed for bear." He fiddled with the straps on his own gas mask. "I just hope Luther Harkin appreciates all the trouble we're going to on his account."

Drastically reducing speed, Tanner brought the Bell down mere yards from the tail of a news chopper. He immediately killed the power and was out the door before the rotors stopped spinning. Bending low, he ran in a zigzag pattern toward the front gate. The other members of Executive Protection, Incorporated mimicked him.

They were halfway there when Tanner caught a whiff of smoke and spotted a man near another copter, smoking a cigarette. He stopped on a dime and raised his right forearm, his fist clenched. The others took that as their cue to flatten.

The smoker wore a cap and jacket typical of a pilot. He was idly watching the goings-on at the gate, the cap pushed back on his head.

Tanner crept to the left. Hugging his knapsack close to his chest, he wound past several more choppers. A row of bushes provided convenient cover less than twenty feet from the crowd. Hunkering, he noted the positions of the nearest National Guardsmen on perimeter duty along the fence.

It was approaching the top of the hour, and several news crews were about to go live with updates. A newswoman was preening in a small mirror held by an assistant. Nearby a middle-aged newsman was practicing his intro. Cameramen fussed with their equipment and checked their lighting.

Tanner nodded at his companions, then donned his gas mask. Opening the knapsack, he took out five cylindrical canisters made of rolled steel. On each was imprinted: M7A3 RIOT CS. He handed one to each of his teammates and kept the rest for himself.

There was a minor commotion at the gate. A man and a woman had stepped out. The reporters flocked to them like vultures to carrion, a score or more asking questions all at once.

"Ladies and gentleman," the man declared, raising his hands for quiet, "I have no new information to impart at this time other than the work crews expect to have the power restored any time now."

A woman shoved a microphone at him. "Mr. Pratt, any word on when you will send a team down?"

"By dawn at the latest." Pratt pointed at a newsman who had raised his hand. "You there. You have a question?"

"Have you heard from the people trapped below? They must be going crazy after all this time."

"It can't be helped," Pratt responded. "Our priority is containment and decon. Slow and easy is the order of the day. If we go rushing in half-cocked, we might unleash a biological genie from a bottle. And once out, we might never be able to put it back."

"Has there been any pressure put on you by Harkin Industries to find Luther Harkin?" another reporter asked.

Tanner didn't listen to Pratt's reply. He motioned at Sax and Romero, tapped his watch, then held up three fingers. They nodded, looked at their watches and crept off through the bushes toward the fence.

Burt Anderson was fingering his canister with an air of regret. "I wish you would reconsider," he whispered.

"We're past that point," Tanner said curtly. "Be ready on my cue."

The reporters switched their attention to the young woman beside Pratt. She began detailing the damage done to the electrical and communications systems. "Every surge protector and fuse was blown out, and half the wiring was fried to a crisp. It's a reminder that for all our fail-safes, all our planning and modern technology, no system is ever foolproof."

"One minute," Tanner whispered to Anderson.

"Accidents happen," the woman stated. "Mother Nature throws tantrums all the time. Hurricanes, hailstorms, tornadoes, thunderstorms. We're no closer to controlling Nature than we were in the Stone Age."

More hands were raised, and several reporters threw questions at her.

"Thirty seconds," Tanner whispered. He held the riot control grenade in his right hand, his thumb firmly over the arming sleeve. He removed the safety pin and gave the nod. Then, taking several swift steps to the edge of the bushes, he rolled the canister toward the crowd. They were all looking toward the pair at the gate, and they were making so much noise, no one noticed.

Anderson did likewise. Over by the fence, Sax and Romero were rolling their canisters toward the National Guardsmen.

As soon as the grenades were released, their delay elements began to burn. Within split seconds of one another, the detonators burst, rupturing the canisters and spewing the CS filler into the air. Rapidly spreading clouds formed, each over five yards in circumference. Reporters and cameramen started coughing and wheezing, and many cried out in fear. Those in the thick of the chemical clouds staggered or fell to their knees, while those not yet affected shoved one another to escape the writhing tendrils of gas.

"It's the biotoxin!" someone screamed.

At that, panic spread like a prairie fire.

Several National Guardsmen were down, gagging and choking. Others raced from the south to help but the spreading clouds brought them to a halt.

Romero and Sax rejoined Tanner and Anderson. In a compact phalanx they dashed into the nearest cloud, their gas masks enabling them to breathe where no one else could. Reporters littered the ground like so many leaves. Some were coughing uncontrollably, some were retching.

Tanner vaulted a woman thrashing madly about. He avoided a man who grabbed at his leg.

The clouds were overlapping. It was child's play for them to reach the open gate unnoticed.

Once they were through, Tanner tossed his second canister. As the CS spurted, he led the way at a sprint to the main building. No one challenged them. No one tried to stop them. Confusion ran rampant.

The doors wouldn't open. Undaunted, Tanner jogged around the corner. A side door was also secure, but not for long. Stepping back, he triggered a dozen rounds into the lock, the suppressor on his MP-5 SD-3 reducing the blasts to quiet coughs.

They needed the aid of pencil flashlights to navigate the lobby. At the elevators, Tanner fished in his knapsack and produced a titanium crowbar, which he applied to one of the doors. Sax lent a hand, and they pried the door wide enough for the four of them to slip inside.

Tanner squatted and looped his hands together. "Up you go," he said, and boosted Romero to the emergency access panel in the ceiling of the elevator car.

Romero opened it and hauled himself up. Lowering an arm, he helped each of them in turn onto the roof.

Stepping to the edge, Anderson peered down into the inky depths of the shaft. "It's still not too late to change our minds," he said.

Tanner was removing military rappelling gear from his knapsack, including a rope, a harness, carabiners and descenders. "Enough, already. Get with the program. Everything will work out fine. Wait and see."

THE EXECUTIONER WAS never prone to a condition known in common parlance as the "heebie-jeebies." First and foremost, in training and temperament, he was a soldier; his mind, like his body, had been honed to a razor's edge. He placed a high premium on clear, crisp logical thinking. Things that went bump in the night never fazed him, because he knew there was always a rational explanation.

Even so, even knowing the berserkers were the result of bioengineering gone haywire, Bolan couldn't stop his skin from crawling as he stared at the dozens of slavering, red-eyed horrors in the corridor. Their fingers made obscene squeaking sounds on the glass. From their throats gushed guttural growls and wolfish howls.

"Bloody hell!" David McCarter exclaimed.

Luther Harkin was cringing against the file cabinet, his fear almost palpable. "Keep them out! Don't let those lunatics near me!"

A renewed onslaught on the door spurred Bolan into turning to the leader of Phoenix Force. "Catch," he said, and tossed McCarter his flashlight. "Get Chandler to the back of the room. I'll hold off the crazies as best I can." Unzipping his biohazard suit, he ejected the Beretta's partially spent magazine and slid it into an inner pocket, then slapped home a fresh one. He folded down the grip in front of the trigger guard, checked that the fire selector was set on the one lone white dot for single shot, and braced for the attack.

It came a heartbeat later.

A chair struck the window with a tremendous crash and glass rained in a torrent. The berserkers yipped and yowled and surged forward, each striving to be the first into the room. In their rabid haste they jostled one another.

The door shook to the greatest blow yet. A blow so powerful, the hinges were ripped from their mountings and the door caved inward. Over it streamed more crazies, their mouths agape, some spattered with gore and blood from previous kills.

Bolan took them as they came, a shot to the head apiece. Seven of the intruders died, but the rest never slowed. They converged in a living wall, blocking off any hope of escape.

The Executioner wouldn't flee if he could. Not when there were Carolyn Edmunds and Bryce Chandler to think of. Bolan continued killing the creatures as quickly as he could. They pitched to the floor, one atop the other, delaying the rest and permitting him to back up a couple of steps to have more space to maneuver.

The din they raised was amplified by the close confines. It seemed as if a thousand vocal cords were roaring and screeching and yipping all at once. The two-legged beasts creating the uproar would stop at nothing until they had ripped their prey limb from limb.

Bolan wasn't about to let them. Thirteen of the magazine's twenty rounds had been expended, yet he had barely made a dent in the berserkers.

Backpedaling, Bolan ejected the magazine and replaced it with the last of his full ones.

Again the berserkers rushed him. Again the soldier met them with a blistering hailstorm. Four, five, six fell, yet still they came, still they howled and drooled and strove to reach him.

Suddenly McCarter was at Bolan's elbow, the Glock in one hand, the two flashlights in the other. He shone the twin beams at their red-eyed faces and took swift aim.

But a strange thing happened. Many of the berserkers in the front ranks recoiled, blinking furiously. Some averted their heads entirely.

"I'll be damned!" McCarter dashed closer, practically shoving the flashlights in their faces.

Bolan understood now why the crazies had held off attacking in the stairwell. They couldn't stand bright light. The drug seemed to have rendered their eyes extremely sensitive. It wasn't much of an advantage, but the wily Briton was exploiting it fully and the berserkers were hastily retreating.

The soldier saw one attacker try to get at McCarter from the side, and he stroked the Beretta's trigger. Another squatted and grabbed at McCarter's ankles. A 9 mm Parabellum mangler dissuaded him.

At that juncture Carolyn Edmunds screamed.

Bolan whirled. Bryce Chandler was locked in combat with a berserker who had one hand clamped onto Edmunds's blouse. Somehow the man-brute had made it past Bolan and McCarter.

Bolan fixed a hasty bead on the back of the attacker's head, but just then Chandler hauled on his foe's arm and tore the offending hand off Edmunds. Chandler and the berserker spun completely around.

The soldier glanced at McCarter. He was driving the last

few crazed lab workers out into the corridor. Bolan returned his attention to Chandler.

The madman had slammed Chandler against the file cabinet and was slowly but inexorably lowering his teeth toward the man's exposed throat. Luther Harkin didn't even try to help.

As swift as lightning, Bolan fired twice. He didn't wait for the berserker to fall. Pivoting to cover McCarter, he was just in time to plant a slug in the temple of a drooling woman who was slinking toward the Briton unnoticed. He downed another in the act of scrabbling out the window. The remainder melted into the shadows.

McCarter halted shy of the doorway. Mustering a grin, he wagged the flashlights. "Let there be light!" he proclaimed.

Bolan hastened to Bryce Chandler, who had collapsed on the floor and was writhing in agony.

Edmunds knelt and tried to grip Chandler's hand, but he pulled loose and rolled onto his side, his teeth clenched.

"Where does it hurt?" Bolan asked. There were no new external wounds that he could see.

"Inside," Chandler said. "I think a few ribs are cracked."

"Hang on. We'll see about binding you up." Bolan surveyed the bodies for signs of life. Only when he was satisfied they were indeed dead did he sit on the desk and eject the Beretta's magazine. It was half empty. Sliding the other clips from his pocket, he thumbed out the unused cartridges. There were enough left to almost fill one mag.

McCarter was splashing a flashlight beam up and down the hallway. "I don't see the buggers. They must have gone off to lick their wounds," he said. He extended one of the flashlights to Bolan. "I believe this is yours."

Bolan trained it on Chandler, who now had the knuckles of both hands pressed to his mouth.

Scanning the room, Bolan realized a lab coat on a rack in the corner was just the item they needed. Retrieving it, he remembered a pair of scissors he had seen in the top drawer of the desk. In short order he had cut four wide strips of cloth long enough to wrap around Chandler's torso.

Edmunds insisted on doing the honors. She eased off Chandler's jacket, wadded it up and slipped it under his head for a pillow.

Luther Harkin swaggered over as she was applying the first strip. "Now will you listen to me when I tell you that the only smart option we have is to make it to the surface? We can't hold off another attack, and you know it."

When Bolan failed to reply, Harkin poked him in the shoulder. "I'm talking to you, damn it."

"Leave him alone," David McCarter said with unmistakable menace.

"Or what?" Harkin demanded. "Exactly what in hell do you think you're going to do?"

"Just this." The Briton slugged him in the mouth.

15

"I don't like this," Burt Anderson said, the words slightly muffled by his gas mask. "I don't like this one bit."

Sax was peering into a fully stocked laboratory. The beam of his flashlight illuminated work tables and an electron microscope. It revealed racks of test tubes, vials and beakers, along with other sophisticated equipment the purpose of which they couldn't begin to guess. But there was one thing it didn't reveal. "There's no one in here, either," Sax said.

"Where is everybody?" Romero was pacing from one side of the corridor to the other like a jungle cat that did not like being penned in. "We've searched almost this entire floor and haven't found a soul."

All eyes turned to Tanner, who tried to hide his confusion but failed. "All right. I admit this isn't what I expected. But that doesn't mean we're giving up. Our client is down here somewhere, and we're not leaving without him. We'll check the final two rooms, then head down to the next level." He strode off, saying gruffly, "Move it, people. You know the drill."

Anderson brought up the rear, watching their backs. Nothing moved behind them. The place was as dead as a morgue. Yet the newscasts claimed well over a hundred workers had been trapped underground.

Suddenly, from the depths of the facility, rose a hellish howl, a long, drawn-out ululating cry made all the more unnerving by the fact that it had undeniably issued from a human throat.

"Madre de Dios!" Romero breathed. "What in the name of God was that?"

The sound was repeated. Anderson's premonition of impending disaster grew worse. "Whatever it is, I don't want any part of it," he stated.

Sax fingered his MP-5. "This rescue mission of ours is turning weird, boys and girls. I'm beginning to think you were right all this time, Burt, and we're in over our heads. Maybe we should bail while the bailing is good."

Tanner's anger was evident. "Listen to the three of you! Since when does EPI leave a job half finished? We've come this far, we'll see it through to the end," he ordered.

"Didn't you hear that thing?" Romero was incredulous.

"Sure, I heard it. There's a dog down here. So what?"

"That didn't sound like no dog to me," Romero said. "I'll stick this out if you want, but I think we're making a mistake."

"Unbelievable," Tanner said in disgust. "I never thought I'd live to see the day when all of you would turn into a bunch of candy asses." He came to a door and angrily flung it open. "Keep this up and you're liable to—" Tanner stopped in midsentence.

"Liable to what?" Anderson prompted. When there was no reply, he and the others moved forward.

Shock hit them like a slap in the face.

The room was a conference room. An oval mahogany table took up most of the space. Bodies lay strewed across it, under it, beside it. Twenty or more, men and women, young and old. Most had been mutilated to the point where their next of kin would never recognize them. Blood was everywhere: in puddles on the table, in pools on the carpet, splattered thick on the walls, spots on the ceiling.

Anderson's gut did flip-flops. "What could have done this?" He thought of the howl they had heard and shuddered.

Sax swiveled, his SMG tucked against his side. "Whatever

it was must still be down here. And it might decide to come after us next."

Romero crossed himself. "We should get out of here. This is more than a rescue mission now."

"No, that's *exactly* what it is." Tanner entered the conference room and nudged a corpse. "No biotoxin did this. Something flesh and blood was to blame. Something we can kill."

"You're not serious," Anderson said.

"Never more so," Tanner vowed. "Harkin will be doubly grateful when we bail his fat out of the fire. He'll praise us to high heaven to anyone who will listen."

"You hope," Sax muttered.

Tanner didn't hear him. "Think of it, boys! We'll be heroes! We'll be on every talk show in the country. New clients will be beating down the door to sign up. It will be all we've ever hoped for."

"Provided the government doesn't throw us behind bars for ten years for this little stunt," Anderson dryly remarked.

"Harkin will use his influence to keep the Feds off our backs," Tanner told them. "He wields a lot of clout in high places."

Anderson swapped glances with the others. He could tell they shared his reservations but as usual they left it up to him to say what was on all of their minds.

"Let's consider a few things. First, we have no guarantee Harkin will stick up for us. If the Feds decide to nail us to the wall, he might back off to avoid bad publicity," Anderson reasoned with Tanner.

"Good point," Sax chimed in.

"Second, and more importantly, we have no idea what we're getting ourselves into. Whatever slaughtered these people might be more than we can handle."

Tanner cradled his MP-5. "You never give up, do you? You've been against this from the start, and you're using every excuse that comes along to shoot holes in it."

Anderson pointed at the bodies. "I just don't want something to *eat* holes in us. Damn it, Tanner, you're not thinking straight. You see this as our jump to the big leagues, when all it might be is a jump into our graves."

"Fellas," Romero said, but they paid him no mind.

"Do you know what your problem is?" Tanner told Anderson. "You've become soft. You're not the kick-butt soldier you once were. You've forgotten how to take danger in stride."

"Fellas?" Romero said again.

Anderson was literally growing hot under the collar. "You're right. I'm not the same man I was when we met. I'm older. I'm wiser. And I know when I'm in over my head."

Romero stepped between them and pointed down the corridor. "I want to know what *that* is!"

A vague figure had appeared out of the murk. All four of them swung their flashlights toward it, but it was too far off to make out much detail other than it stood on two legs.

"What can it be?" Romero whispered.

"A person, what else?" Tanner took several steps. "You there! We mean you no harm! We're with Executive Protection, Incorporated."

Whoever it was shuffled a few feet closer, then stopped.

"We're looking for Luther Harkin," Tanner hollered. "Can you tell us where to find him?"

There was no response.

Sax leaned forward. "Is it me, or are that sucker's eyes red?"

"You're imagining things," Tanner said, and tried again. "My name is Ike Tanner. These are my business associates. Identify yourself, please."

Still, the figure said nothing.

"I think it's a woman," Romero said.

Anderson agreed. She had shoulder length hair and wore a lab smock, but there was something very strange about her. Her posture, for one thing. She was slumped forward as if she were ill. And maybe his mind was playing tricks on him, but he'd swear Sax was right; her eyes were glowing preternaturally red.

"Didn't you hear me?" Tanner bellowed. "You have no cause to be afraid. We won't harm you."

The woman shambled into full sight, moving with a bizarre stiff-legged gait. Her face was like a mask, and she had drawn her lips back from her teeth like a wild animal. She blinked repeatedly and raised a hand to shield her eyes.

"What the hell is wrong with her?" Sax wondered.

Anderson was as mystified as everyone else. "If I didn't know better, I'd swear she was going to attack us," he warned.

The next moment that was exactly what the woman did. Howling fiercely, she sprinted toward them with astounding speed.

THE BROKEN DOOR MADE an excellent stretcher. Bolan and McCarter exercised great care as they slid Bryce Chandler onto it. McCarter took one end, Luther Harkin took the other, and they started down the corridor in search of a safe haven.

Harkin hadn't said a word since the Briton had punched him. Like a petulant child, he had sulked until Bolan ordered him to help. Even then, he glared in blatant spite and wasn't particularly careful about jostling Chandler.

Edmunds had hold of the NSA man's hand. "Hang in there," she encouraged him. "As soon as the lockdown is lifted, we'll rush you to a hospital."

Chandler smiled, but his heart wasn't in it. He was terribly pale, and sweat covered him like a second skin.

Bolan had talked it over with McCarter and had reached a reluctant decision. One of them had to stay behind. Edmunds and Chandler stood little hope of surviving on their own, not with killers hovering in the shadows, waiting for another opportunity to strike. Bolan could hear some moving about in the dark that very moment.

A closed door yielded to a twist of the knob. It was another office, larger than the last, with a long row of file cabinets along the right wall. The cabinets gave Bolan an idea. Pushing the door as wide as it would go, he motioned for McCarter and Harkin to carry Chandler inside.

Edmunds paused, anxiety shrouding her like a mantle of doom. "Those things won't hold them off forever, will they?"

"The lights are bound to come back on eventually. They'll be easy to subdue then." Bolan had avoided the direct question, since the answer was transparent and there was no sense in compounding her worry.

McCarter steered the stretcher to a bare spot and gently lowered his end down. Harkin wasn't nearly as considerate and let go when the door was still a couple of inches off the floor. It hit with a thump.

Bryce Chandler swore. "If I make it out of this alive, Luther, I'll be paying you a visit as soon as I recover."

"I'm trembling in my socks." Harkin broke his silence and walked over to a chair to do more sulking.

Bolan beckoned to McCarter. "If you lose this, you owe me a new one." He held out the Beretta.

"I take it you've decided to go after Hal yourself?" The Phoenix Force leader made no move to accept the pistol. "Why you and not me?"

"I've known him longer," Bolan stated.

"Granted. But what will you use to fight off the beastie brigade? Spitballs?" McCarter shook his head. "Keep it. I'll make do.'"

The soldier lowered his voice. "You have people to protect. I don't. You'll need it more than I will." He shoved the Beretta into the Englishman's hand. "Remember to go for the head."

Phoenix Force's leader plainly didn't like it. "I'm doing this under protest. And only on one condition. We swap." He pulled the Glock from his belt. "There are eight rounds left."

Bolan accepted it without argument and stepped to the door.

Too much time had already been squandered. "I recommend stacking file cabinets against the door and window," he said.

"My thinking exactly." McCarter followed Bolan out and surprised him by offering his hand. "It's been a pleasure, Mack. I mean that sincerely."

"You make it sound like we'll never see each other again." Bolan shook his comrade's hand, then spun and broke into a run. He flashed his light over every doorway and window he approached to foil a potential ambush.

The stairwell was eerily still. Bolan descended rapidly but noiselessly, his flashlight cutting a brilliant swath out of the gloom. He passed the landing to Sublevel 9 without incident, then Sublevel 10. Midway to 11 he stopped. Shoes had scuffed on a step below. Leaning over the rail, he splayed the beam downward. What he saw was enough to spawn nightmares for eternity.

A knot of figures were hunched over a body at the bottom. They were clawing and tearing at it like a pack of drooling hyenas. The moment the light struck them, they raised their arms over their eyes and scurried under the stairs. Except for one.

Bolan rested his right arm on the rail. Compensating for the elevation and angle, he fired. His target keeled over with a grunt. Bolan resumed his descent, only to stop in his tracks as a chilling realization knifed through him: the body at the bottom of the stairs was about the same height and weight as Brognola.

"Not like that!" Bolan declared, and went down the stairs on the fly. Three crazies moved to meet him, but he shot them before they could set foot on the lowest step. He saw the victim's face and halted, flooded by relief. Enough remained to show it wasn't his friend.

Like a stalking panther, Bolan sidled to Sublevel 12. Growls and hisses warned him the berserkers under the stairs would be after him as soon as the dark enveloped them again. With only four rounds left, it would be folly to confront them unless he had no choice.

Bolan pushed through the doorway. He was tempted to shout Brognola's name, but it would only alert other crazies to his presence. Going from doorway to doorway, he sought some sign of his friend.

The soldier was not one to bare his feelings in public. But the truth was, he had stuck with the Feds as long as he had in large part because of his respect and admiration for Brognola. By nature Bolan was a loner. Even during his military days, as a sniper he had spent weeks on his own in the field. Later, when he launched his War Everlasting, he had waged it alone for the longest time. He did everything his own way. And he had been supremely effective. So much so, the government approached him with their offer. They would stop hunting him, would stop trying to put him behind bars if he agreed to work with them and wage the war on their terms.

Bolan had agreed, but not because he trusted them. He joined the Stony Man program because it gave him access to intel and hardware he could never access on his own. Still, he'd had to make a major attitude adjustment.

Hal Brognola had made that adjustment easier. The big Fed not only earned Bolan's respect and admiration, he earned something far more rare. Brognola was one of the few people Bolan unreservedly trusted. Were it not for Brognola, Bolan might not have stuck it out as long as he had.

Brognola had always been there when Bolan needed him. Not just on the many ops they waged together, but where it mattered more, on a personal level. Bolan knew he could go to Brognola with anything, and the Fed would move heaven and earth to help him. Even now, after he struck out on his own and had an arm's length relationship with the government.

So here Bolan was, deep in a quarantined research facility, risking his life to save that of one of the few people he called friend.

A noise drew the Executioner toward an open door. He was a few yards from it when a shadow filled the doorway. Pressing his back to the wall, he switched off his flashlight. A solitary emergency light at the far end of the corridor cast enough feeble glow for him to distinguish the shuffling shape that emerged and turned toward him. He let it take a couple of steps, then switched on his flashlight again.

The bright beam caught the infected man full in the face and it averted its eyes. Snarling, it groped forward.

Bolan shot it smack in the center of its forehead and moved on. He was down to three rounds.

A noise behind him alerted him that the stairwell door was opening. He turned his flashlight on it and the door swung shut. But the crazies wouldn't hold off forever. If he didn't find Brognola soon there would be hell to pay.

The next room Bolan checked was Lab 24. The place looked like a tornado had ripped through it. Cabinets had been knocked over, their contents strewed wildly about. Every beaker and container had been thrown down, and broken glass layered the floor like a carpet. Bolan came to a shattered partition. Beyond it was a spacious chamber. Mutilated bodies were scattered amid busted chairs.

Bolan was about to turn when he noticed that several of the fallen men wore uniforms. He remembered Barbara Price telling him that some of the VIPs were military brass. Stepping closer, he bent over a Marine. The insignia and name tag identified the deceased as a General Drake.

In a far corner something crunched.

The Executioner whipped around in a crouch. His beam revealed three ghastly shapes on their haunches beside another body. They reared up, their mouths rimmed red, and shuffled toward him, moving slower than he had ever seen the attackers move.

Bolan started to back away, thinking they wouldn't attack as long as he held the light on them.

But he was wrong.

16

David McCarter didn't much like being separated from Bolan. They had worked well together. Left on their own, it lessened their chances of success, and he was not one to deliberately buck the odds.

McCarter had always been a team player. True, he had an independent streak a mile wide and a temper he had to constantly keep under control. But he also had a knack for meshing with others. The SAS had recognized his talent. So had Hal Brognola. It was because of Brognola that he had become head of Phoenix Force. McCarter was happy to repay the favor any way he could, even if it meant putting his life on the line.

Another positive trait was McCarter's devotion to his friends. He would do anything for a mate. In his estimation, loyalty was an earmark of maturity. Any man who wouldn't stick by others in need was no man at all.

Luther Harkin was an excellent example of what McCarter despised. He wouldn't stop pacing, wouldn't stop complaining. "He's going to get us killed, I tell you. We should be on our way to the surface, not stuck here minding someone who can't stand on his own two feet."

"Quit your griping!" Edmunds said. She was seated next to Chandler, her hand holding his.

The NSA man was a lot worse off than before. Sweat beaded his brow, and he tossed and turned in a dazed delirium.

"I speak my peace," Harkin said flatly. "Always have, always will. You don't become a captain of industry by being timid."

Edmunds laid into him with both barrels. "No, you become one by stepping on others as if they were bugs. By not caring who you hurt in your rise to the top. By always, and I do mean *always,* putting yourself ahead of everyone else."

"You make that sound like a crime." Harkin smirked. "But it's men like me, my dear, men with ambition and drive, who have made this country of ours as great as it is."

"There are a lot of decent industry leaders out there, too," she argued. "Men who care about those who work for them. Men who wouldn't abandon a sinking ship before the women and children."

"Sticks and stones," Harkin said smugly.

McCarter had put up with all he was going to. "That's enough out of you. I can't hear the loons for your blathering."

Harkin rubbed the spot on his jaw where McCarter's fist had connected earlier, and turned away in a huff.

"I'm worried about Mr. Chandler," Edmunds said to Mc-Carter. "He's so hot, it feels as if he's on fire. He must have a temperature of 110. Can't we find something for him to drink? Water, maybe? Or a can of soda?"

"There's a pop machine three doors down on the left," Harkin said. "But don't expect me to go. Those things could be anywhere."

Edmunds started to rise. "I'll do it," she said.

"No, if anyone should go, it should be me," McCarter said. "I can be there and back in three shakes of a lamb's tail." He read the woman's anxiety and added, "Don't worry. I'll keep one eye on this room. If those Frankensteins show themselves, they'll be sorry."

"Go ahead, then," she said. "But please watch yourself."

McCarter wouldn't do otherwise. Flicking the flashlight both ways, he passed the first room, then the second, knowing attackers might spring out from anywhere dark. He glanced back repeatedly.

Luther Harkin was in the office doorway, smiling enigmatically. He gave a little wave.

McCarter didn't return it. The third room was only a few feet away. Slowing, he saw that it was as black as tar inside. He speared his flashlight beam into it and heard a growl. A responding growl came from farther down the corridor. McCarter began to back up, but the damage had been done.

Biofreaks emerged from two rooms. Both moved slowly, their faces severely drawn and haggard. But they were as fierce as usual and, on spotting him, they hissed and charged.

McCarter dropped each with a single shot. He had to use his remaining ammo wisely. Sixteen more, and the magazine would be empty.

A roar suddenly reverberated, like that of a bear about to go amok. A brawny specimen in a security guard's uniform was thrusting both huge arms out in front of him and hurtling down the hall like a runaway train. He was fast, incredibly fast, and McCarter almost didn't get off his shot in time.

The slug spun the madman but didn't stop him. Roaring anew, he took two loping strides.

McCarter squeezed off a second and third shot but the security guard took another lumbering step, his sweaty palms a fraction of an inch from McCarter's throat. The Briton fired one last time.

The security guard hit the floor with a thud.

McCarter heard the slap of footsteps and spun. He thought it was another crazy, but it was Luther Harkin moving in full flight toward the stairwell. "Come back, you bloody fool!" McCarter shouted.

Cackling with glee, Harkin reached the stairwell door and looked back. "I told you I always look out for number one! You'd be wise to do the same!" He waved again and was gone.

"Good riddance to bad rubbish," the Phoenix Force leader

said under his breath. If anyone deserved to be caught by the berserkers, it was Harkin. They would be doing the world a favor.

McCarter ran to the office. "Are the two of you all right in here?" It took a few seconds for what he was seeing to register. When it did, he drew back against the jamb. "No!" he breathed.

Bryce Chandler was up on one knee, his thick fingers wrapped tight around Carolyn Edmunds's neck. The whites of his eyes had turned scarlet, and his lips were curled back from his teeth.

Edmunds's lifeless gaze was fixed on the ceiling. The tip of her tongue protruded from her mouth, which was parted in a scream she had never uttered.

"I was only gone a minute," McCarter said softly.

The thing that had been Bryce Chandler cast Edmunds aside and lurched toward him, snarling.

The Beretta banged once. McCarter stared a moment, wheeled and jogged toward the stairs.

THE EXECUTIONER WAS a qualified marksman with a handgun, a rifle and an SMG. He had spent countless hours on the target range, almost as many in combat. His expertise and reflexes were second to none. Yet as quick and as sure as he was, he dropped only two of the charging horrors. Then the third was on him in a flurry of flailing limbs and fingers hooked to rend and rip. A blow caught him across the shoulder, catapulting him into a row of chairs. His legs became ensnared and he fell—hard.

The assailant didn't give him a moment's respite.

Bolan had one round left in the Glock. He pointed it at the bridge of the madman's nose, but as his finger tightened a flying chair smashed against his arm. The pistol discharged its lethal lead into the ceiling, and a second later the crazed manbrute had Bolan by the front of his biosuit, lifted him as if he were weightless and threw him at the wall.

The man's strength was prodigious. Bolan crashed onto the floor and felt as if his chest were on fire. He slid his hands under him to push to his feet and felt steely fingers clamp onto the back of his suit. Again he was lifted into the air. Again he was thrown with ridiculous ease.

This time Bolan hit on his shoulder and slid into a broken chair. One of the smashed legs, tapered to a sharp tip, filled his vision. He scooped it up as the steely fingers once again gripped his biosuit. Bunching his shoulder muscles, he twisted and lanced the chair leg into the attacker's left eye.

For all their ferocity, for all their chemically enhanced might, the crazies were as mortal as their intended victims. The chair leg sheared into the socket like a hot knife into wax. Letting go, the madman grabbed it and attempted to wrench it out. But it was too deeply imbedded. He took a halting step, then withered in a heap.

Bolan was a shade sluggish in rising. He hurt all over. Every bone, every muscle ached. His biosuit had been torn in half a dozen spots. He reached up to touch it and saw a fine sheen of sweat that wasn't his. Undoing the zipper, he carefully peeled off the biosuit and left it.

The empty Glock was of no use, but Bolan retrieved it and stuck it in his shoulder holster anyway. He also reclaimed his flashlight, which thankfully still worked. Moving back into the lab, he searched for something to use to defend himself. In the gloom near the front was a closet he hadn't noticed before.

The soldier's fingers were a hair's-width from the knob when he heard what sounded like a hiss coming from the other side. He started to back off, then realized it hadn't been a hiss, after all. It was whispering.

Bolan yanked the door open. A hand grasping a syringe flashed at his neck, but he blocked it and said, "I'm happy to see you, too."

Hal Brognola's astonishment turned him to stone. His mouth moved but no words came out.

"Who is it?" someone else asked. "Move so I can see!"

Like a sleepwalker in a trance, the big Fed slowly emerged, lowering the syringe.

From behind him stepped a smartly dressed young woman who took one look at Bolan in combat black and blurted, "They sent a hit man to save us?"

"He's a friend of mine," Brognola said, and put a hand on Bolan's shoulder. "I won't ask you what you're doing here. All I'll say is that you shouldn't be." His forehead furrowed. "Please tell me you received clearance from upstairs first."

Bolan clasped Brognola's wrist. "How could we? Without you, we had to wing it."

"I was afraid of that." Brognola looked around. "Then please tell me you came alone."

"I brought along a certain feisty Brit," Bolan replied.

"Really?" Brognola grinned. "I'm surprised the facility is still standing." The big Fed looked Bolan in the eyes. "I will never forget this. Even if it costs my job."

The woman had her hands on her hips. "I don't suppose either of you would care to fill me in on what this is all about?"

"Maybe later. Oh, before I forget, Ms. Lucy Reese, meet my friend, Striker." Brognola did a double take. "Wait a minute. You didn't think to wear a hazard suit? And where are your weapons? You never go anywhere without an armory."

"It's a long story." Bolan motioned for silence. Something was happening out in the corridor. Gliding past them, he peeked out. Berserkers were filing through the stairwell door. He counted six in all, moving with that peculiar shambling gait of theirs. "We've got company," he warned the others.

"Back into the closet," Lucy Reese said.

Bolan did not want to be cooped up if he could help it. He liked having room to move, to fight or flee as the case might be.

"What are you waiting for?" Reese demanded when he hesitated. "We've been hiding in there a good long while, and they haven't found us yet." She was facing toward the VIP lounge, and she suddenly gasped and stiffened.

Bolan knew what he would see before he turned. A madman was at the shattered partition. It lifted a leg but lowered it again and began trembling. The drool oozing from its mouth changed to greenish froth.

"What the hell!" Brognola exclaimed.

"Remember what Dr. Bellamy told us?" Lucy whispered. "About these things burning themselves out? Maybe that's what we're witnessing."

But the abomination was far from dead. It stopped trembling and lumbered forward, sweat dripping from it in a steady shower.

"If that thing gets so much as one drop on us…" Brognola left the thought unfinished.

"Stick close to me," Bolan said, and dashed into the hallway. The crazies howled and flew toward him, but his flashlight brought them to a frustrated halt. They hissed like a nest of serpents as he retreated with Brognola and Reese on either side.

"Where can we go?" Reese asked. "There's nowhere we can run to that they won't follow!"

A room on the left was nearest. Bolan gave it a swift scrutiny. It wasn't a lab, it wasn't an office, but a combination of both, with a desk on one side and a table covered with chemical apparatus on the other. "In here." He slammed the door and worked the lock. Then, grabbing a chair from behind the desk, he wedged it fast just as the first blow landed.

Lucy Reese swallowed hard. "This was a mistake! They'll break that down before we know it."

"Maybe. Maybe not." Bolan ran to the table. "Give me a hand," he said to Brognola. Sweeping the apparatus onto the floor, they lifted the table and pressed the top flat against the door, then put their backs to it to hold it in place.

"Maybe the phone works," Reese said as she snatched up the receiver. Her frown was eloquent testimony to the fact it was still out of order.

More blows rained, accompanied by yowls and screeches. Bolan felt the table start to give and dug in his soles.

Brognola's jaw was set in grim lines. "I still can't believe you did this. Barb and Aaron should have talked you out of it."

"Who do you think helped me work out the logistics?" Bolan said with a grin.

That was all either of them could say for a while. The uproar became deafening as the berserkers lived up to their nickname and assaulted the door in a paroxysm of animal outrage. The door jumped on its hinges, despite the extra support, and several times Bolan was sure it would cave in.

Lucy Reese, meanwhile, was rummaging through every drawer and cabinet in the place. She found several knives, a hammer and a microscope hefty enough to use as a club, and brought them over.

Bolan chose the hammer. To use it he would have to get in close, but it was better than nothing. A row of canisters on a shelf also looked promising. One was labeled Sulphuric Acid.

Suddenly the howling stopped, the pounding ended. Half a minute went by without a sound.

"Shouldn't we take a look and see what they're up to?" Reese said.

The soldier shook his head. It might be a ruse.

"Where is that British friend of ours, by the way?" Brognola inquired. "We can use all the help we can get."

Bolan told him about Bryce Chandler and the others. "They'll hang tight until we get there." Or so he hoped. David McCarter wasn't always the most patient of soldiers.

Minutes dragged by without a peep out of the walking horrors. Bolan began to think that maybe it wasn't a ruse. Maybe the berserkers had gone elsewhere. Straightening, he wedged the hammer under his belt and took hold of the table. "Both of you stand back," he said.

Brognola was dubious. "Why push our luck?"

"David and our friend are waiting on us," Bolan replied.

They slid the table far enough from the door for him to unlock it. Every nerve tingling, the Executioner turned the knob. He saw no one. Encouraged, he widened the gap enough to stick his head out.

The instant he did, a clammy hand touched his neck.

17

Gloria Stenger was having the worst day of her life. It wasn't bad enough that Richard Pratt was lording over her like she was his personal servant. It wasn't bad enough Director Benjamin was upset with her for allowing the two doctors from the CDC to go below, and would arrive at the Spider Mountain Research Facility within the hour to take personal command. And it wasn't bad enough the repair crews *still* didn't have the phone lines up or the power restored. She had a new problem: someone had penetrated the site after tossing tear gas to create confusion and sow panic.

"They shot out the lock?" she said in disbelief.

"Yes, ma'am," Colonel Williams of the 29th Infantry Division of the Virginian Army National Guard confirmed. "I thought I should bring it to your attention right away. Should I inform Mr. Pratt, or will you?" he asked.

Stenger gazed toward the gate where her immediate superior was conducting yet another interview. "Leave that to me. Secure the door and double the guards around the main building, if you would be so kind."

"Consider it done, ma'am." Colonel Williams did an about-face and marched off to do her bidding.

Stenger was at a total loss. Why anyone in their right mind would want to break *into* a quarantined facility was beyond her.

The TV crews and print journalists were having a field day with it, speculating terrorists were to blame. Pratt had nipped their sensationalism in the bud by claiming the tear gas had been dispersed by mistake as part of a practice drill. For once, he had done something right.

But when all was said and done, Stenger's main worry wasn't the break-in, or the power situation, or even the director's imminent arrival. The thing she was most concerned about was the welfare of the doctors from the CDC. They had been below much too long. If they had come to harm, the blame would fall squarely on her shoulders. She should never have let them sweet-talk her into giving permission.

Stenger headed for Annex D. Enough was enough. She had to get the ball rolling or the next thing to roll might be her head off her shoulders. She had too much time and energy invested in her career to sit idly by while it collapsed around her.

The workmen were bustling about like bees in a hive. Stenger walked up to the electrician in the Virginia Tech cap and flatly stated, "I want power restored in fifteen minutes or else."

"Fifteen minutes it is, lady," he replied without looking up from a meter he was reading.

The woman couldn't hide her surprise. "You're not putting me on?"

"Nope. We're almost set to go. There's still a lot of burned wiring to replace, but we've rigged a bypass that will give you full power. Lights, elevators, the whole she-bang." He winked. "A dozen roses and a thank-you card, and I'll consider us even."

Laughing for the first time in more hours than she could recall, Stenger said, "I want to be here when you throw the switch."

"You got it," the electrician promised.

Stenger was halfway across the compound when she saw Richard Pratt jogging toward her like a runaway locomotive. Judging by his flushed face and the thunder crackling on his brow, she figured she was in for another lecture on her general incompetence.

"I just received word from a buddy of mine at the home

office," Pratt announced. "You're never going to guess who is on his way here even as we speak!"

Feigning ignorance, Stenger responded, "I have no idea."

"Director Benjamin! He must be coming to check on us. I want everything up to snuff when he arrives. I need to make a good impression."

"I'm sure you will, sir," Stenger said with a straight face.

BARBARA PRICE DIDN'T realize Kurtzman had come up beside her until she removed her headset and stretched to relieve a kink in her back. "Bear! You're making a habit out of sneaking up on me."

"And you're making a habit out of working yourself to death." Kurtzman set a BLT on a plate on the console. "I figured you could use a bite to eat, since you didn't have supper."

"Keep mothering me like this and it will go to my head." Price treated herself to a bite and chewed with enthusiasm. "I'm starved. Keeping tabs on an op like this takes a lot out of a person."

"It would take a lot less if you wouldn't shoulder so much of the work yourself. That's what we have a communication crew for."

Kurtzman nodded at the headset. "What's the latest? Is Jack en route with the packages yet?"

Price's cheerful facade evaporated. "Still no sign of our guys. Jack was all set to climb out and nose around when there was some sort of commotion. He saw four guys in black land a chopper and make a beeline for the front gate. The next thing he knew, people were screaming and running for their lives."

"From what?" Kurtzman asked, alarmed.

"Tear gas. Now the National Guard has doubled the number of perimeter guards. They're also conducting regular patrols of the surrounding area."

Kurtzman read between the lines. "Which will make it twice as hard for Mack and David to get Hal out of there."

"When it rains, it pours," Price replied. "A VDEM director by the name of Joshua Benjamin has been on the horn to the CDC. He knows Mack and David aren't legit, and he's on his way there to get to the bottom of it."

"How long before this Benjamin arrives?"

Price consulted the wall clock. "His connecting flight was delayed, so he won't show up for another forty minutes yet."

"That doesn't give our boys much time." Kurtzman was thoughtful for a moment. "Any chance in delaying Benjamin even more?"

"We can't intervene directly or it might raise eyebrows," Price replied.

Kurtzman scratched his chin. "Is Benjamin on a government jet or a civilian flight?"

"Civilian. Due into Washington, D.C., on a flight out of Richmond. From there he's taking a helicopter to Spider Mountain."

"What if the airline were to receive an anonymous tip that terrorists are planning to blow it up when it lands? That might delay it awhile, don't you think?" Kurtzman suggested.

"It would also delay everyone else on board," Price noted. "Need I mention that our mission is to safeguard civilians, not inconvenience them?"

"What's a little inconvenience if it saves lives? Think of all the sacrifices Striker has made. Don't you think we owe it to him to pull out all the stops on this one?"

"You've sold me." Price picked up her headset and grinned. "You're positively wicked when you want to be."

"Now you know why women find me so irresistible," Kurtzman said, laughing.

THE FOUR MEMBERS of Executive Protection, Incorporated held their fire until the last possible moment. Tanner yelled at the woman to stop, but his warning fell on deaf ears. She was only a few yards away when he triggered a shot into her right shoulder that spun her like a top. "Now maybe you'll listen to reason," he shouted.

But the red-eyed harpy did no such thing. Screeching, she threw herself at them again, heedless of her wound and the blood seeping from it.

This time it was Sax who squeezed off a 3-round burst that stitched her chest and hurled her against the wall. "That should stop her," he said, shaken.

"She acted like she was on angel dust," Romero remarked. "What the hell has been going on down here?"

They passed the crumpled heap that had been the red-eyed woman. An inhuman shriek brought them to a halt with their weapons leveled. But they didn't fire. They were frozen in horror and shock by the sight of the woman rising to her feet and baring her teeth in a hideous hiss.

"It can't be!" Sax declared. "I killed her! You all saw it!"

For a dead woman she was remarkably agile. A lithe bound carried her to them. She kicked Romero, knocking him down, and attacked Sax. Before he could finish what he had started, her fingernails dug furrows in his neck deep enough to draw blood.

Romero yelled and cut loose on full-auto from a prone position on the floor. His MP-5 turned the woman into a sieve, yet she still didn't die. She had absorbed enough lead to kill ten men, but hissed and came at them again.

"What does it take to finish her off?" Tanner's eyes were as wide as walnuts.

Burt Anderson met her rush by jamming the muzzle of his SMG against her temple and splattering her brains to kingdom come. She deflated like a punctured balloon. "That's what it takes," he declared, as shaken as the rest, and glanced at Tanner. "*Now* will you believe me when I say we're in over our heads?"

Tanner's face mirrored uncertainty. But they all knew how stubborn he could be, and now was no exception. "I'll admit this isn't going as planned. But we can't call it quits until we've found Harkin," he said.

Sax was wiping his sleeve across the gashes in his neck. "The hell we can't. What if there are more like her?"

"We blow them away, too." Tanner moved on, but much more cautiously than before.

Burt Anderson brought up the rear again, but this time he wasn't alone. Sax hung back, still wiping off blood, and extremely upset.

"What the hell has gotten into our fearless leader? Is he trying to get all of us planted six feet under?" Sax asked.

"All he sees are dollar signs," Anderson said. "He's always wanted EPI to play in the big leagues."

"I know that," Sax snapped. "But this isn't the way to do it. We should leave something like this to the experts."

"What have I been saying all along?" Anderson replied.

Sax seemed not to hear. "I mean, that woman was stone cold psycho. Did you see her frigging eyes? And how she took all that lead and kept getting back up? It's not natural, man."

Anderson glanced over his shoulder, sure he had heard a footstep. But no one was there.

Sax wouldn't let it drop. "I have half a mind to tell Tanner to take a flying leap, and split. It'll piss him off but I don't care." He stopped and half turned. "Did you hear something?"

"Yes." Anderson nudged him. "Keep moving. It might be more of those things, whatever they are."

Flipping the selector switch on his MP-5, Sax patted the SMG. "Next time one of those suckers shows its ugly face, I'm turning it into dog food."

Tanner reached the stairwell and motioned for quiet. He slowly opened the door, then signaled the coast was clear. They joined him on the landing. Their small flashlights alleviated some of the murk but not enough. From out of the shadows came furtive sounds that did not bode well.

Anderson and Sax looked at each other, and Sax muttered a few choice profanities.

"Stay frosty, gentlemen," Tanner advised, and started down.

"Frosty?" Sax repeated sarcastically. "If I were any frostier, I'd be an icicle."

At Sublevel 2 Tanner halted. "We'll pair off and go from room to room. Burt and I will take the right side. Sax, you and Romero take the left. Watch each other's back." He pushed on into the corridor but had taken only a couple of steps when muted popping from somewhere below brought him back to the landing. "Those were shots!"

Romero sprang to the railing. "It's a regular firefight!"

"Sure as hell is." Sax ran over, too. "Somebody is up against more of those freaks, I bet."

Tanner moved to the next flight of stairs. "It must be Harkin and his security people. No one else would have guns down here. Let's hustle. They might need our help."

"It could be anyone," Anderson quickly countered. "We're asking for trouble if we go racing down there without knowing what we're getting into."

"Slow and safe won't save Luther Harkin." Tanner hurried lower. "If I have to, I'll do this myself."

Romero promptly followed.

"Damn them," Sax said. But he wouldn't desert Tanner, and down he ran.

Only Anderson gave pause, and only for a few seconds. "God help us," he said softly, and took the stairs two at a time.

No more shots rang out but that didn't dissuade Tanner from leading them steadily lower until they were at the landing to Sublevel 9. He listened at the corridor, as he had at the others. "I don't hear a thing. They must be lower," he said.

"You're taking too much for granted," Anderson warned. "Let's play it safe and hold here until we know for sure."

Tanner shook his head in reproach. "You used to be someone I could count on through thick and thin. Now you've turned into my grandmother."

"*¡Silencio!*" Romero suddenly whispered.

Footsteps rang on the metal stairs; the source was climbing toward them. At a gesture from Tanner they ranged across the landing, their flashlights trained on the top step.

Raspy breaths and erratic footfalls convinced Anderson it had to be another lunatic. But the head and shoulders that appeared were a godsend.

"Mr. Harkin!"

The industrialist sagged against the rail. "Who the——" He blinked in bewilderment and noisily sucked air into his lungs. "Are you the military?" he asked.

"No, sir." Tanner rose and removed his gas mask. "Executive Protection, Incorporated, at your service. Fulfilling our end of the contract you have with our agency." He stood at attention as if he were still in the military and Harkin were his commander.

"EPI?" Luther Harkin straightened and glared. "It's about damn time! I expected you hours ago!"

"We came as soon as we could, sir," Tanner said. "You have no idea of the difficulties we've encountered."

"I pay you to surmount difficulties, not to use them as excuses." Harkin poked Tanner in the chest. "I could have been killed ten times over since the lockdown went into effect. Out of the goodness of my heart, though, I'll overlook your lapse if you get me topside."

"That's why we're here," Tanner said. "But with the power down we can't use the elevators. And the National Guard will have all the exits covered. So our only option is to make it onto the roof and lower ourselves down by rope."

"There's another way," Harkin said. "A utility tunnel on Sublevel 6 that very few people know about. I can show you where it is. Just give me a minute to catch my breath."

"Take all the time you want," Tanner said, brownnosing.

"You'll be pleased to hear there is no extra charge for this rescue. It's all part of the package."

"It had damn well better be. You're lucky you showed up or I'd have sued you for breach of contract."

A rumbling growl filled the stairwell. On its heels came another, then a third, along with the scrape of shoes on the stairs. A lot of shoes.

Tanner leaned out over the edge. "Good God! Get behind us, Mr. Harkin! We'll do our best to protect you."

Anderson had to see for himself.

Out of the dark they slunk. Dozens of them. Scores. A small army of red-eyed demons who now threw back their heads and howled.

18

The Executioner reacted automatically. He threw himself to the left and swept the hammer over his head, prepared to bash out the brains of the berserker before it could do him in. Only it wasn't a drooling madman. It was a grinning Englishman.

"If I'd been the Real McCoy, as you Yanks like to say, your neck would be crushed to a pulp and I'd be treating myself to a Bolan burger right about now," David McCarter said.

While the Executioner was glad it wasn't an attacker, he was also puzzled. "Don't take this wrong, but what are you doing here?" He gazed down the empty hall. "You're supposed to be guarding the others."

McCarter's features clouded. "Chandler changed into one of those zombies and killed Carolyn. There was nothing I could do."

"And Harkin? Wasn't he with you, too?" This came from Hal Brognola, who had emerged from Lab 24 with Lucy Reese.

"He's almost to the surface by now, would be my guess," McCarter said. "Which is where we should be heading."

"Have you seen any berserkers?" Reese nervously asked.

"Dozens, but I was able to avoid them," the Phoenix Force leader stated. "Most were heading up the stairs. With any luck, they'll give Mr. Luther Harkin a taste of his own well-deserved medicine."

"Let's go, then," Bolan said. He took a step but had the Beretta thrust at him, butt first.

"I believe this is yours." McCarter wagged it. "I'll trade you for that hammer. And I won't take no for an answer."

The Briton was sacrificing the edge the pistol gave him, a gesture that wasn't lost on Bolan. "Stay behind me. If I go down, do what you can to save Hal and the lady," Bolan told him.

Just then Lucy Reese cried out.

Bolan whirled and beheld a pair of crazies moving toward them. He snapped up the Beretta and had the first in his sights when he realized something was wrong with them.

Both moved more stiffly and awkwardly than usual. Instead of drool dribbling over their chins, they were frothing at the mouth like rabid dogs. As the soldier watched, the foremost aberration broke into convulsions. It fell onto its side and thrashed about like a fish out of water. The other berserker tried to step over the first, but their legs became entangled and it toppled. Seconds later it was bucking and heaving as if in the grip of an epileptic fit.

"They've burned themselves out, just like that other one!" Lucy Reese grimaced. "What a horrible way to go."

"Let's hope they all burn out," Bolan said. He would rather avoid another clash if he could.

He figured he would find more berserkers at the bottom of the stairs but there were none. Scuffling from higher up compelled him to point his flashlight overhead.

Dozens of crazies were several stories above, and climbing higher.

"It looks like a mass exodus!" Brognola whispered. "Where could they be going?"

"There's your answer!" Reese exclaimed.

The beams of several flashlights were splashing over the stairwell and the walls. Someone else was up there, someone still human. Someone the abominations were about to attack. The next instant a new sound filtered down, the faint but unmistakable chug of SMGs outfitted with sound suppressors.

McCarter cocked his head. "The National Guard, you think? Or maybe Harkin's security people?"

"There's one way to find out." Bolan climbed rapidly, but not so fast as to outdistance Brognola and Lucy Reese. Twice he had to slow down so they could catch up. Above them the battle raged unchecked, a crescendo of fiendish cries and howls mixed with the chug of autofire and the random curses of men caught up in the heat of conflict.

Suddenly a lone voice shrieked clear and loud, "Stop them! Don't let them touch me! *Don't let them touch me!*"

Reese paused. "That was Luther Harkin!"

Bolan looked up. For a fraction of a second he was riveted by what he saw then he dived toward her. Clamping his free arm around her waist, he pulled her to the landing. They landed hard, scraped and bruised, but it couldn't be helped. Not if he was to save her life.

Reese squealed in surprise and pushed at his shoulders, then went rigid as a body crashed onto the landing in the exact spot where she had been standing. It struck with such force, the entire landing shook.

The soldier rolled off her and onto his knees. By rights, the person who fell should be dead. Any normal person would be. But not the berserker. Another drooling travesty of all that was human—a man in his mid to late thirties—who sat up and hissed and didn't seem to notice that half his chest was caved in. Gleaming bone jutted from the twisted wreck that had once been his right arm.

The creature spotted Brognola and lunged.

Bolan raised the Beretta but David McCarter beat him to the punch. The Briton stepped up close behind the loathsome horror and brought the hammer down on the crown of its head. The berserker shook spasmodically, then collapsed in a lifeless sprawl.

High above the conflict continued to rage. Crazies lay in heaps on the stairs yet their numbers were barely dented.

They flowed onto the landing like a tidal wave onto a shore. A hailstorm of lead chopped them down as soon as they showed themselves, but for every one that fell, there were two to take its place.

"Whoever it is, they're putting up a hell of a fight," McCarter said in admiration.

Bolan climbed faster. They were a few steps short of Sublevel 10's landing when a tremendous explosion rocked the stairwell. "Hit the deck!" he yelled, and flattened, throwing his hands over his head.

Debris rained down. Bits and chunks of the stairs and the masonry, along with bits and chunks of human bodies. A falling section of railing gouged Bolan's shoulder. A fist-sized piece of concrete missed his head by inches. Then came swirling tendrils of dust that coalesced into a choking cloud.

The soft chugs of more autofire showed the firefight wasn't over.

Pushing erect, Bolan checked on his companions. McCarter was unhurt. Brognola had a deep cut above his right ear. Lucy Reese was bleeding from one cheek. "What was that?" she asked in a daze.

"A grenade." Bolan steered her to the next flight of stairs. "Can you make it on your own?"

"I'll take care of her," Brognola volunteered. "The two of you go on ahead. Whoever is up there might need all the help they can get."

Bolan was loathe to leave them, but Brognola was right. "Keep your eyes peeled and don't lag behind," he said.

Shoulder to shoulder with McCarter, he bounded upward. He had to skirt a lot of bodies to reach the next landing, but that was nothing compared to the landing itself.

Berserkers were stacked in heaps like so many cords of firewood, their craniums perforated by slug after slug. It was impossible to reach the other side without stepping on them.

"I'll go first," Bolan said, and clambered onto the pile. He used care in not brushing against exposed skin. There were so many, a distinctly uneasy feeling gripped him. Everywhere he looked, a grotesque face stared back. He made sure each spot he stepped would bear his weight before lifting his other leg.

The howls and feral cries from the next landing abruptly died. So did the chug of SMGs.

Boots thudded overhead. Bolan steadied his flashlight and saw several figures in black and another in a suit hastening upward. They had to notice his flashlight, but they didn't stop or call down to him. The reason became clear when he heard Luther Harkin bellow.

"Hurry up, damn you! Get me out of here while you still can! There might be a few of those things left!"

Taking hold of the rail, Bolan hauled himself over the largest pile of bodies yet, and finally reached the site of the firefight. Here the dead were four and five deep. Body parts were strewed at random, especially within the blast radius of the grenade. Whoever rescued Harkin had made their stand at the base of the next flight of stairs, and held firm against all odds.

Bolan's beam bathed a black-garbed figure on the fifth step up. A small, wiry Hispanic man had both arms over his belly and was doubled over, motionless. Bolan couldn't tell whether the man was alive or dead until he got closer.

The man's head snapped up. He extended a Browning BDM pistol clutched in an unsteady hand soaked with blood and gore. Pain-racked brown eyes narrowed, and he said weakly, "You're not one of those things!"

"I'm Dr. Brown from the CDC," Bolan said as he pressed a finger to the Browning's barrel and pushed it aside. "We heard the shooting and came as fast as we could."

"My name is Romero." The man gazed at the slaughter. "They wouldn't stop coming. We killed them and killed them, but there were always more. We dropped them in waves, but it was never enough."

Bolan indicated the man's stomach. "How bad are you?"

"Any moment now. That's why I told my friends to leave me." Romero forced a lopsided grin. "Never thought I would buy the farm like this, amigo. Gutted by a damn ghoul." He rested his head against the rail. "They were right on top of us, and one got hold of my boot knife." He laughed as if a great joke had been played on him. "Can you believe it? Killed with my own knife!"

McCarter came up next to Bolan. "Where are the rest?"

"Taking Harkin out," Romero said weakly. "Two of them were hurt or they would have carried me."

"Are you with Harkin Security?" Bolan asked.

"No, Doctor. EPI." Romero smiled proudly. "Executive Protection, Incorporated. Harkin is one of our clients."

"I'm surprised the VDEM gave you permission to come down here," McCarter said.

Romero's laugh was more in the nature of a death rattle. "We did this on our own, hombre. Now they're escorting Harkin to D.C. He wants to lie low and avoid the media for a while."

Bolan had a troubling thought. "They're taking him to Washington straight from Spider Mountain?"

"Yes. Harkin is offering a bonus of a hundred thousand dollars if they get him there with no one the wiser." Romero's smile faded. "I will never get to enjoy my share." His eyes closed and he mumbled, "Harkin knows a secret way out."

McCarter glanced at Bolan. "The utility tunnel, you reckon?"

But the soldier was thinking of something else, something with potentially dire consequences for the entire country, if not the world. He shook Romero's shoulder until Romero's eyelids fluttered open.

"What is it, Doctor? I am tired."

"Did the ghouls touch any of your friends?"

"Touch them, Doctor?" Romero tried to straighten but couldn't. "I am not sure I understand. We fought them with all we had. With our guns, with our knives." He paused. "With our fists."

"Bloody hell," McCarter said.

Bolan twisted to inform Brognola, but there was no sign of the big Fed or Lucy Reese. "Hal?" he called out.

"We're coming!" was the reply. "It's taking us a while to get past all these bodies!"

They couldn't afford to wait. Too much was at stake. Bolan turned to McCarter, who nodded. "What are you waiting for? I know what has to be done. Get cracking, mate, before that jackass brings about the end of civilization as we know it."

It was no exaggeration. Should the unthinkable occur, should the biotoxin be unleashed in a major urban center like the nation's capital, there might be no stopping it. By morning there could be thousands of berserkers. Within twenty-four hours, hundreds of thousands.

Bolan had to see to it that Luther Harkin and the EPI team didn't leave the Spider Mountain Research Facility. No matter what it took. He started up the stairs but stopped after a few steps and tossed the Beretta to McCarter, who caught it without half trying. "You might need this more than I do." Especially if there were any berserkers left. It would take quite a while for Brognola and Reese to reach the airlock, and they would be in danger every step of the way. So would he, but he was extremely proficient at hand-to-hand combat and they weren't.

"Bust Harkin in the chops for me," the Briton said.

The industrialist and the EPI team were climbing like bats out of hell. They had to be close to Sublevel 6, or at it.

Bolan pumped his legs, using the rail for extra leverage. He remembered to stay alert for crazies but saw none until he was crossing the landing to Sublevel 7. It was in the shadows, frothing and quaking, and paid no attention to him whatsoever.

The soldier was almost to Sublevel 6 when, without fore-warning, the lights came back on. One second it was pitch-black except for his flashlight, the next, it was so bright, the glare made him squint. A loud hum and the whir of electronic circuits told him the power had been restored. "About time," he said to himself, and doubled his speed.

Bolan was spurred by a mental image of hordes of crazies swarming through the streets of Washington. The police would be overrun, and troops would be called in to impose martial law. But would that be enough? He doubted it. Infected individuals would run riot through the countryside, and there weren't enough troops available on short notice to quarantine the entire District of Columbia, let alone the surrounding states.

The soldier finally reached Sublevel 6. He sprinted down the hall, avoiding a berserker who flapped about in the final stages of burnout. Soon his worst fear was borne out. The airlock door hung wide open.

Bolan had never liked Luther Harkin. The man was a financial tyrant who lorded it over his underlings and looked down his nose at those he deemed his inferiors. It was no secret Harkin always put his personal welfare before all else. But not until that moment had Bolan fully appreciated just how selfish and self-absorbed the tycoon truly was. All Harkin cared about was getting out of there. The lives of those who might become infected were of no consequence to him.

The soldier wondered what the EPI men were thinking, to endanger so many for the sake of one man. As he sped along the utility tunnel, it dawned on him that maybe the EPI team didn't know that contact with a berserker was all it took to spread the biotoxin. It would be just like Harkin not to tell them if it served Harkin's own ends.

Bolan was running flat out, but there was no sign of his quarry. Soon he spied the inner door to the airlock in Annex D. It, too, had been left wide open. He hoped against hope that Harkin and the EPI team hadn't made it out the other side of the airlock, but they had already gone through and were out of sight.

Desperation lent wings to Bolan's feet. He was through the airlock before he saw the young National Guardsman crumpled on the floor. He stopped just long enough to confirm the Guardsman was alive, then ran down the long aisle between the generators, past startled technicians and out into the cool of the night.

Twenty feet away was Gloria Stenger, walking toward Annex A. She heard him and turned. "Dr. Brown! I was just about to report to Mr. Pratt that the power has been restored."

"Did you see them?" Bolan asked.

Stenger was more interested in him. "Where's your biosuit? And what happened to Dr. Clancy?" she asked.

"He'll be along shortly." Bolan scoured the compound, asking again, "Did you see them?"

"See who?" Gloria asked.

"Luther Harkin and several other men." Bolan's frustration was mounting by the second. They had to be there somewhere.

"No, I sure haven't. But I have been on the phone with Director Benjamin, and he's on his way here to take personal command."

Bolan couldn't have cared less. He jogged toward the front gate. He didn't see how Harkin and EPI had snuck out of the generator building without being noticed but apparently they had. Which meant they would try to make it through the gate at any moment.

The ranks of the newsmen and camera crews had swelled. Four National Guardsmen were supposed to prevent unauthorized personnel from entering, but it never occurred to them that unauthorized personnel might try to leave. The gate had been left open wide enough for Luther Harkin to bolt through with the EPI crew hard on his heels. They were among the media before the National Guardsmen could think to stop them.

"You there, halt!" a sergeant belatedly bawled, with no more effect than if he had waved feathers in their faces.

Bolan shouldered two of the Guardsmen aside and was also among the crowd before they could recover. He had to push and shove to make headway. The sergeant was bellowing like a mad bull, but all he was doing was adding to the growing commotion and confusion.

Luther Harkin was also bellowing. "Out of our way! Move, damn it!" His three black-suited rescuers had formed a wedge around him and were plowing through the media like a Spartan phalanx through the Persians.

Bolan lost more ground than he gained. Reporters and other media personnel kept blocking his way. Someone inside the fence barked orders, and he glanced back to see an officer leading half a dozen Guardsmen into the thick of things in pursuit.

Bolan was glad to note that the members of EPI were wearing gloves. It might prevent spread of the biotoxin if any of them were infected. But one of them was bleeding, and it was likely blood could transmit the condition as effectively as sweat.

Harkin and his bodyguards broke into the clear and ran in among the whirlybirds. Bolan tried to keep track of them, but being jostled constantly and with shadows blanketing the aircraft, it was a hopeless proposition. He had five or six yards to go when a black helicopter rose on gossamer blades, banked sharply and streaked to the east.

Luther Harkin had done it. And in so doing, Harkin now posed the greatest threat to civilization since the bubonic plague.

19

Jack Grimaldi was talking into his headset when the Executioner jerked open the door of the helicopter. Grimaldi covered the mouthpiece and said, "About time you got back! Barb is ready to have a cow, and Aaron is none too happy, either." He peered past Bolan. "Where's the big guy and Mr. Bloody Hell?"

The soldier hauled himself inside. "Get this bird into the air and follow the copter that just left!"

"Oh, goody. Some action." Grimaldi began flicking switches. "Care to fill me in?"

Briefly, Bolan did, while the rotors spun faster and faster and a low whine filled the cockpit. He concluded with, "We have to stop them by any means necessary. Even if the only way is to crash into their chopper."

"A kamikaze mission?" Grimaldi chuckled. "Even better. Although it will lose something in the translation. We need a real Zero."

Bolan was in no mood for his friend's warped sense of humor. "They'll be halfway to D.C. before we get off the ground," he said.

"O, ye of little faith," Grimaldi replied, and rose into the air so steeply they were slammed back against their seats. "Do you think I would fly just *any* helicopter? This baby has been souped to the max, and then some. Hang on to your false teeth." With that, he streaked toward the horizon.

"You added armament, I hope," Bolan said. It would simplify matters greatly.

"It's rigged for speed, not warfare. Sorry," Grimaldi said.

Rolling mountains canopied in forest flashed by underneath. Bolan had eyes only for a blinking light approximately a mile ahead. "Raise Barbara. Tell her to have an F-16 scrambled in case we fail."

"Wash your mouth out with soap. Failure isn't in my vocabulary. And it sure as blazes isn't in yours," Grimaldi retorted.

"It never hurts to have a contingency plan," Bolan reminded him. Especially with so much at stake.

"Roger that." Grimaldi raised Stony Man Farm.

Afterward, they flew in tense silence, save for the whir of the blades and the throb of the engine. Bit by bit they closed the distance. Bolan would have given anything for an air-to-air missile or a nose-mounted M-134 minigun. He was absorbed in mulling the best means of bringing the other chopper down when his friend poked his arm.

"Take a gander at the Bell."

The other helicopter was swinging from side to side, like a pendulum at the end of a string. It abruptly climbed straight up, then just as abruptly dipped a good fifty feet. Suddenly it streaked along above the treetops, flying so low it was a wonder the copter's undercarriage wasn't scraping the upper branches.

"Five will get you ten they're looking for a spot to land," Grimaldi said. "They must be having mechanical trouble."

"Or some other kind." The kind Bolan was thinking of held dire consequences for all of them if it wasn't contained.

"That pilot is a nutcase," Grimaldi said.

The Bell was darting back and forth like a frenzied dragonfly. It climbed again, then veered southeast at a high rate of speed.

In a display of supreme skill, Grimaldi paced the other craft with flawless precision. They were now within a couple of hundred yards. The other chopper began swaying back and forth like a boat tossed in a storm-swept sea.

"If I had to make a guess, I'd say someone was fighting the pilot for control of the stick," Grimaldi said.

Someone? Bolan reflected. Or a red-eyed wildman?

"Look. There's a clearing yonder."

The Bell's pilot had apparently spotted it too, because the next moment the Bell plummeted toward it at suicidal speed.

"They're going to crash."

No sooner were the words out of Grimaldi's mouth than the other copter hit the ground. The impact buckled the frame and bent the tail. Bolan hoped that Harkin and the others had been knocked out; it would make his job that much easier. But he saw the passenger-side door fly open and an inky figure limped off into the darkness. Seconds later a second figure emerged. This one moved with a stiff-legged gait the soldier had witnessed too many times already that day.

"Take us down," Bolan directed. "As soon as I'm out, you're to dust off and stay in the air until I signal."

"You're going after those two guys alone? What am I, chopped liver?" Grimaldi patted his side. "It's not as if I haven't shot enough lowlifes to fill Yankee Stadium."

"I need your piece." Bolan held out his hand.

"Anyone ever mention that you have a bossy streak?" Grimaldi said as he handed over the pistol, then concentrated on landing.

It was a SIG-Sauer P-220. Swiss-designed but German-made, SIGs were considered some of the best pistols in the world. A 9 mm, it had enough stopping power to take down a normal man with no problem, but Bolan knew the berserkers weren't normal.

"Hey, what do you make of that?" Grimaldi pointed.

A mile to the south were several small fires. Campfires, Bolan figured. Since hunting season wasn't for months yet, he doubted they were hunters. And since there weren't any lakes or rivers nearby, it couldn't be fishermen. "Backpackers, maybe, on a wilderness hike," he said.

Grimaldi touched down as light as a feather. "Be careful, Sarge." He lifted off again the second Bolan was out the door.

The Bell resembled a broken toy. Much of the tail assembly lay on the ground. A spiderweb of cracks latticed the cockpit, and the door was crumpled like an accordion. The engine was dead, but the cockpit glowed with instrument lights that dimly bathed the slumped form of the pilot.

Bolan worked the SIG's slide to feed a round into the chamber. Holding the pistol in one hand and his flashlight in the other, he edged closer. The pilot didn't move, even when Bolan poked him with the flashlight. A mangled neck explained why.

Another body was on the floor between the seats. A stocky man with sandy crew cut hair lay in a spreading pool of blood.

About to turn away, Bolan saw the man's eyes open. They were white, not red, and awash in agony. The man spotted him and tried to rise onto his elbows. "I saw you at Spider Mountain!" he croaked. "You were chasing us."

"That was me," Bolan admitted.

"You've got to stop him. Stop Sax. He's out there, somewhere. And he's no longer human."

Bolan remembered the one who had been bleeding from the neck. "Sax is the black guy?" Bolan asked.

The man was barely able to nod. "One of those things clawed him. That must be all it took." He glanced at the dead pilot. "Poor Tanner. So much for his big idea." Leaning against the other seat, he groaned. "My name is Burt Anderson. We didn't know about those things when we went in. Honest to God we didn't."

"Luther Harkin didn't warn you about not letting them touch you?"

"That bastard?" Anderson was fading rapidly. "All he cares about is his own hide. Now I know why he insisted Sax sit in the back with me. He knew the whole time." Anderson sighed and lowered his cheek to the floor. "I told them this was a bad setup. I told them we were out of our league. But do you think they would listen?"

With that, he died.

An MP-5 lay behind the pilot's seat. Bolan reached for it, then thought better of the idea. It might belong to Sax, and anything that belonged to him might have his sweat on it.

In the distance the campfires blazed. That was the direction Harkin had gone, Sax too, probably, Bolan mused, and jogged into the trees. He listened for a few seconds but heard only the leaves rustling in the stiff breeze.

Plunging into the undergrowth, the soldier moved as swiftly as the dark and the terrain allowed. It was an unsettling feeling, knowing that somewhere out there lurked a creature created by science gone wrong. A monster that would attack without hesitation or mercy, and with the unique ability to turn everyone it touched into a carbon copy of itself.

For hundreds of yards the forest was unbroken. Then Bolan came to a gully. At the bottom gurgled a creek. He descended a short grassy incline, leaped to the other side and started up the facing slope. He would never know what made him glance to his left. Whether it was a whisper of movement or pure instinct. But whatever it was, it saved his life.

A shadow had detached itself from the night. Bolan twisted aside but had the flashlight knocked from his grasp. The apparition that rose to confront him was nearly invisible against the backdrop of night. He didn't see the hand that clawed at his neck until it was inches from his throat.

Jerking aside, Bolan leveled the pistol but Sax was faster. An iron arm clipped Bolan on the shoulder and sent him tumbling. He ended up on his back in the creek. A snarl heralded Sax's next attack. The soldier rolled upright and snapped off a shot at the man's head, but had to have missed.

Bolan ducked under a blow aimed at his face. He dodged

to the left, dodged to the right. Sax never relented, never gave him a breather. Backpedaling, Bolan fired twice at near point-blank range.

The berserker tottered, sank onto one knee and pitched forward.

The flashlight was a few feet away, on the creek bank. Bolan retrieved it and cautiously rolled the prone form over. His slugs were spaced a fraction apart above the right eyebrow.

There was no time to lose. Scrambling up the south bank, the soldier settled into a dogtrot. It was hard to say how much of a lead Luther Harkin had by now, but he was confident it wouldn't take long to overtake him. Harkin wasn't all that physically fit, while Bolan always kept himself in peak condition.

But Bolan ate up the distance, and the yards stretched into half a mile. Then three-quarters of a mile. Bolan began to wonder. The forest was littered with logs and boulders, as well as thickets and other pockets of heavy brush. Low limbs also had to be avoided. They slowed him down but not enough to account for why he hadn't caught up yet. Harkin was either in a lot better shape than he thought, or there was another, much more sinister reason.

The three campfires were situated on a hill where they were visible for miles. Maybe, if Bolan was right, the thing Harkin had become sensed that where there were campfires, there would be prey.

Bolan came to the base of the hill. A sound reached his ears. It took a few seconds for what he was hearing to register, and when it did, he threw all caution aside and raced upward with reckless regard for his own welfare.

Dozens of children were singing "Row, Row, Row Your Boat."

The soldier fairly flew. Soon he glimpsed their camp off through the trees. Scouts in uniform, the same color his had been when he was their age. Some were roasting marshmallows on sticks.

An accident of fate had placed them in the wrong place at the worst of times. Bolan imagined Harkin circling them, waiting for a chance to grab one. "Watch out!" he bellowed in warning. "You're in danger!" He saw a scoutmaster rise and gesture for quiet, but most of the scouts didn't notice and kept on signing.

"Get those kids into the tents!" Bolan shouted. It wasn't much, but it might delay Harkin a few seconds, and a few seconds were all he needed.

Some of the boys had stopped singing and were looking around in confusion. Another scoutmaster was trying to quiet the rest.

Bolan played his flashlight over the surrounding woods. To his right a pair of red-rimmed eyes blinked at him from behind a tree. He angled toward the tree but when he got there, Harkin was gone.

Pivoting from side to side, Bolan probed the brush. There should be some sign of Harkin, but there wasn't. He couldn't understand it. There hadn't been time for Harkin to go very far.

Then a snarl rent the night, directly above him. Without looking up, Bolan dived away from the tree. He heard the thud of Harkin's feet striking the ground, then the man heaved up into a crouch. His flashlight caught Harkin full in the eyes, forcing the industrialist back a couple of steps.

Few who knew the former captain of industry would have recognized him. His arrogant features were contorted in a bestial mask. The cruel mouth that once could not stop criticizing everyone around him now could not stop leaking drool. Elemental hatred was mirrored in his bloodshot eyes.

Bolan snapped off a shot, but Harkin whipped to one side. The slug that was supposed to core the man's skull cored the tree instead. With a lightning-fast bound, Harkin seized Bolan by both wrists.

The soldier tried not to think of the sweat coating Harkin's palms. He tried not to think of what would happen if it seeped through his blacksuit onto his skin. Twisting his hand, he tried to point the SIG at Harkin's face. But the biodrug had turned Harkin into a Hercules. Not only couldn't Bolan move his hand, but his arms were slowly but inexorably being bent back.

Harkin opened his mouth wider. His intent was plain. He would tear out Bolan's throat with his bare teeth.

The Executioner had other ideas. He let Harkin bend him backward, let his teeth come perilously close to his throat. Then, exerting every sinew he possessed to its limit, he twisted, hooked his right ankle behind Harkin's leg and pushed. It threw Harkin off balance. The vise on Bolan's right wrist slackened just a little, enough for him to wrench his arm free. Instantly, he jammed the gun's muzzle against Harkin's forehead and banged off three shots.

Luther Harkin was flung against the tree. His hands clawed at empty air, his knees caved and he melted to the earth.

It was over.

Bolan inhaled the crisp night air deep into his lungs and wondered how Hal Brognola would explain everything to the President.

Epilogue

Stony Man Farm, Virginia

Barbara Price chaired the meeting. Brognola considered that only fair since she oversaw much of the op at Harkin Industries, with Kurtzman's able input.

"Every member from the various units that responded, from the CDC to the National Guard, have been closely monitored for the past month. Every reporter who was on-site has been watched around the clock. There have been no new reports of biomorphs, as the classified report refers to them," she said.

David McCarter snorted. "Bloody rabid loons, is what they were."

"Not as far as the public is concerned. The official line is that a biotoxin was to blame. No one will ever be the wiser except us and a few others."

"All's well that ends well, is that it?" McCarter retorted. "All those poor bastards lost their lives, and the government sweeps the whole mess under the rug? Bloody typical."

Brognola stirred. "What else would you have the President do? Go public? Congress would raise a hue and cry to have every biopharm in the country shut down. He has to balance the good that comes out of them against this one incident."

Until that moment Bolan had been silent. Now he sat up and asked, "What about Lucy Reese?"

"Like every other CIA employee, she had to sign a confidentiality agreement as a condition of her employment," Brognola said. "She's been sworn to secrecy for the rest of her natural life."

Price was staring at McCarter. "If it helps, the government has given the families of the victims generous financial aid to tide them over."

"Bought them off, in other words," the Briton replied.

"Is something bothering you?" Brognola asked.

McCarter shrugged. "I didn't much like blowing away civilians, is all. It's not in the job description, if you know what I mean."

The Executioner rose and came around the table. "I owe you an apology, David." He offered his hand.

"For what?" McCarter asked suspiciously.

"I didn't think you cared. I thought that to you it was just another op."

"Give me a break, mate. The day I can kill women and old men and not feel a twinge of conscience is the day they should put me out to pasture." McCarter thrust out his hand and shook.

"If that's all?" Bolan said to Brognola, who nodded. "I'm due to meet Cowboy in a few minutes to test a new weapon." He was almost to the door when he stopped and looked at McCarter. "We worked well together, David. You're a credit to Stony Man Farm. You're a hell of a man, and we couldn't have gotten out of there without you." He walked out.

A slow grin spread across David McCarter's face. "Did you hear that?" Rising, he hooked his thumbs in his belt and ambled out of the room, whistling softly.

"All's well that ends well," Price said softly to herself, and smiled.

*Read on and share in the excitement as we celebrate the
remarkable Mack Bolan series with episode #100*
DEVIL'S BARGAIN
*The fuse has been lit, the conspiracy unleashed.
Will America survive?*
DANCING WITH THE DEVIL

Alpha Deep Six. Wetwork specialists so covert, they were
thought dead. Now this paramilitary group of black ops assassins and saboteurs has been resurrected in a conspiracy en-
gineered somewhere in the darkest corners of military
intelligence. Their mission: unleash Armageddon.

They've got America's most determined enemies ready to
jump-start the nightmare, and the countdown has begun.
Blood and terror are poring through America's streets. A presidential directive has cut through red tape, dropped Mack
Bolan square in charge. His orders are clear: abort the enemy's twisted dreams.

If Bolan survives, then it gets really personal. Because
Alpha Deep Six has a hostage. A Stony Man operative...

Available at your favorite bookstore next month.

Prologue

Jaric Muhdal was waiting for the miracle to happen.

Word of the alleged breakout had been written in Kurdish on a wadded note tossed in his lap five days ago by his Turk captor. Muhdal had been ordered to eat the missive once he'd read it. Or was it six days, a week since the encounter? And was this simply mental torture, taunting him with false hopes of escaping the hell on earth called Dyrik Prison? One last sadistic blow by his tormentors to break his spirit, and days, he believed, before he was marched out to the courtyard to be beheaded?

It was nearly impossible to track time or grasp insight into mind games played by his tormentors, he concluded as he hacked out a strand of gummy blood, wincing when his tongue ran over the craters inside his mouth. Rage building, he felt the slime ooze down over his bare chest and stomach, pool to a warm slither against exposed genitals. Time was frozen, but his hatred felt as if it could last an eternity.

How much more could he take? Daily he was hung upside down, pummeled by fists, flogged by a metal studded belt. A slice of moldy bread, a cup of tepid water a day—he was a withered sack of drooping flesh. For endless hours he sat naked and bleeding from his scalp to the soles of his feet in the blackness of a six by four concrete-block cell, breathing the stink of his own filth and fear; waiting for execution. Still, solitary confinement was respite from torture.

He knew plenty about deprivation, suffering, cruelty—his

people, after all, had been savaged by the Turks for eighty years—but even those who believed they carried the heart of a lion could long for death under such brutal conditions.

Only they wouldn't break him, he determined. No begging to be spared when the time came, no crack in the armor of his will. He would take what he knew about his fellow PKK freedom fighters with him to the grave. As leader, there was no other way, the warrior's ego also dictating he stand an iron pillar, an example of unwavering defiance in the enemy's face. With the imprisonment of Abdullah Ocalan, the disappearance of his younger brother, Osman—previous heir to power—he hadn't climbed the ranks of the Workers Party of Kurdistan by showing mercy, either to friend or foe. Why expect anything now but the worst at the hands of a savage, hated enemy? He would die the way he had lived. At worst, he could take comfort not even his death would cripple the dream of a Kurdistan nation.

Muhdal felt the pain dig needles of fire through every nerve ending. For some strange reason agony seared to mind images of his wife and three children, murdered many years ago by Turk soldiers, leaving him to wonder how much they had suffered before they were beheaded, their bodies dumped in a mass grave with the other villagers. The ringing in his ears, his brain jellied and throbbing, smothered by darkness, and he found himself suddenly drifting away into warm darkness. Muffled by the steel door, the screams of other prisoners, whipped and beaten down the corridor, some of them, he knew, with testicles plugged into generators, echoing the cry of anger and hatred in his heart.

Pain was good, he decided. So was hate.

So was never forgetting.

Focus, he told himself, perhaps the Turk was being truthful. Hold on.

"Hope!" Escape first, then dip his hands in more enemy blood. Perhaps freedom was on the way, but at what price?

he wondered. After all, the guard, like many Turks there, he knew, were Boz Kurt, members of a secret netherworld of militants, all of whom were hardly resigned to carry out the Ankara regime's wishes without personal gain. Their treachery and brutal ways were legendary, even by Turk standards. The Gray Wolves—or so went the mythical nonsense, he knew, fighting to pull thoughts together inside the crucible of his skull—believed the first Turk was suckled by a wolf on the Central Asian steppe. Whether or not the milk of a wild beast spawned a bloodline of ferocious warriors, Muhdal only knew all Turks were devils in human skin. As for the Boz Kurt they weren't only considered terrorists by Ankara, but they were also drug traffickers.

Which was why he and fifteen of his fighters had been arrested in the first place.

Revolutions required money to purchase weapons, even loyalty. Briefly he thought back eight months, the Turks catching them asleep, but the question lingered as to how the Turks had found them, slipped so easily into the gorge. Of course, he never expected a trial, a just legal system all but an alien concept in Turkey. His crimes—or so the Turks claimed—ranged from murder to drug trafficking, too many, in fact, to count.

Killing the enemy, he believed, was acceptable in the eyes of God. So was stealing from Turk thieves and murderers, a holy decree, spoken directly to him from God in dreams, telling him the spoils of war were to be used to gain an edge against the enemy. How could he, in all good conscience, have stood idly by anyway, watch the Turks use the southeast corner of the country to fatten their own coffers with truck caravans of heroin funneled from Afghanistan, hashish from Lebanon? And when the Ankara regime, faceless butchers who marched their killers out to Anatolia, had declared a campaign of genocide against them generations ago, and soon after the treacherous Brits reneged on their promise to give the Kurds their own country…?

The groan echoing in his ears, he gnashed chipped, broken teeth, invisible flames racing down the long furrows in his back. It hurt to breathe.

The first of several rumbles sounded from a great distance, but it was next to impossible to judge direction, much less clearly absorb sound through the chiming in his ears, windowless walls and door a barrier to whatever the source. He strained his ears, heart racing, then shuddered to his feet, hand on wall to brace himself. Tremors rippled underfoot next, the thunder pealing closer, nearly on top of his cell. This region, he knew, was notorious for earthquakes, ground splitting open without warning, hills crumbling down to consume tens of thousands within minutes. Images of being buried alive were jumping through his mind, then the bedlam beyond the darkness broke through the bells in his ears.

Muhdal laughed, hope flaming as the racket of weapons fire, the screams of men being shot in the corridor seemed to pound the door, an invisible but living force shouting freedom was mere feet and seconds away.

The murderous din, he thought, oh, but it was the singing of angels.

Freedom! Salvation! Revenge!

He made out the rattling of a key being inserted. Laughing, so giddy with relief, he wasn't sure he could walk. But pain seemed to leak out of bruised and gashed flesh like water through a sieve right then. Waiting, he watched as the door swung out, light stabbing the dark, piercing his eyes, autofire and angry shouts blasting a wave of sense-shattering noise in his face.

Squinting, he made out the stocky figure of the Boz Kurt guard. He was shoving himself off the wall when it happened.

There was a wink of light in the doorway, a shadow rolling up behind the man, an armed wraith clad in black, from hood to boots. Muhdal looked from the bayonet fixed to the assault rifle, believed he heard *tesekkurler,* the hooded one thanking the guard in Turk. Then a pistol flew up in a gloved hand, the shadow jamming the muzzle against the Turk's skull. Muhdal felt his knees buckle as the shot rang out, and blood sprayed his lips.

THE UNIDENTIFIED BOGEY blipped onto the screen, dropping from the sky, out of nowhere, it seemed. By the time he calculated numbers scrolling on the digital readout—speed, distance and rate of descent—Colonel Mustafa Gobruz knew it was too late. The hell with his men assuring him there was no evidence of malfunction. Whatever the object, it was sailing a bullet-straight course for the compound, less than one minute out, he figured, falling to slam right on top of their heads.

Gobruz felt the anxiety edge to panic in the room, his three man radar team crunching numbers he already knew. "I can read!"

The colonel then barked orders to scramble all hands, man the antiaircraft batteries, shoot down the bogey on sight. But even as he punched on the Klaxon to throw the compound into full battle alert, Gobruz feared the worst, doomsday numbers ticking down now to mere seconds. The sprawling compound might survive a direct hit from a missile or a crash landing by a crippled aircraft. The dread concern, however, was for the ammunition depots, fuel bins, choppers, motor pools, every machine in close proximity to the C and C, topped out with fuel and—

One explosion, pounding through ordnance and thousands of gallons of high-octane fuel, he knew, and the base would erupt, a conflagration leaving behind a smoking crater on the east Anatolia steppe.

Gobruz, snapping up field glasses, burst out the door, stared to the southeast. Baffling, frightening questions shot through his mind as he glanced at soldiers racing up behind the big guns, searchlights scissoring white beams over black sky, barracks spilling forth more troops.

This was no accident, he knew. A deliberate attack, no question, but who was manning the craft, plunging it to the base, perhaps using it as a flying bomb? Or was it one of those unmanned drones, maybe packed with high explosives? Again, who, why? The Kurds had no access to either surface-to-surface missiles or aircraft, much less high-tech unmanned aerial vehicles. Of course, Iran, Iraq and Syria bordered the nation, often providing weapons and fighters to the Kurds, hoping the primitive rabble could create its own independent nation, thus invite them in when the Ankara government collapsed.

Gobruz glanced at the antiaircraft guns, soldiers working with a fury to bring the cannons around and on-line. He was lifting the field glasses, but discovered there was no need.

The object was coming to them, hard, fast and low.

The searchlights framed the craft's bulk, not more than a hundred feet up and out, he saw, as it nose-dived for the cyclone fencing. It appeared, a midsize cargo plane, lights out, but no transport bird he knew of carried what appeared to be missiles on its wings.

"Fire!" he shouted across the compound. "What are you waiting for?"

He heard the bark of small-arms fire—why weren't the big guns pounding?—glimpsed the fixed-wing plane clear the fenceline.

Then the world erupted in a flash of roaring fire. Blinded by a white sea of flames, eyeballs and face scorched by superheated wind, Gobruz caught the shrieks, his men torched by incendiary explosions, he was sure. He was wheeling, about to launch himself through the doorway when he felt the flames sweep over him, his own screams added to the chorus of wailing demons as he was consumed by the wave of fire.

"Live or die, your choice!"

Muhdal watched the faceless gunman, unsure of what was even real, senses warped, swollen by the din. Peering into the

bright sheen, Muhdal saw the wraith flash white teeth, dark
eyes burning with either laughter or anger. He strained to listen, his savior telling him he had ten seconds to strip the Turk
and dress, or the door would slam shut.

Some choice, he thought. Outside, the price for freedom
sounded more to him as if the gates of hell had opened to dis-
gorge a legion of devils, there to devour every prisoner.

Men bellowed in agony, wailing from some distance. Muhdal nearly gagged as he sniffed the sickly sweet odor of roasting flesh. Were his men being burned alive, trapped in their
cells, thrashing, craving for death to extinguish their misery?
Were his rescuers Turks or Kurds? What was this madness?

His confusion deepened, as the wraith snapped an order
over his shoulder, switching to the Russian language. Another hooded shadow swept through the doorway and hurled
what he assumed was water from a bucket. Muhdal took the
liquid in the face and chest, then howled when he realized
what doused him. The urine burned like acid, biting into
countless open wounds.

"Bastards! You throw piss in my face?"

"Five seconds, or I shoot you dead!"

Was that laughter in his eyes? Muhdal wondered, the piss-
thrower stepping back, kicking away the Turk's assault rifle,
then melting into the corridor where the hellish noise reached
a deafening crescendo. Cursing, with a bayoneted muzzle
inches from his face, Muhdal nearly shredded the blouse and
pants off the body, dressed, finally squeezing into boots a size
too small. No weapon in his hands, but he felt the gun in his
heart, cocked and ready with murderous wrath, the pain a
scalding blaze, now that urine was smothered by clothing,
soaking into fabric. He was tempted to lunge for the RPK-74
light machine gun, but the hardman grabbed him by the shoulder, snarled something in Russian, shoved him through the
doorway.

"Move it!"

Muhdal found more black hoods swarming the halls. Some were armed with the longer, heavier version of the AK-74, banana clips holding forty-five rounds, Muhdal noting holstered side arms, commando vests, webbing studded with grenades and spare clips, com links snugged over hoods. Two big machine guns, Squad Automatic Weapons with 200-round box magazines in the hands of giants. He figured eight invaders at first count, but with shooting converging from all directions it was impossible to say. The deeper he headed down the corridor, the more he feared his immediate future. Several of the invaders were emptying weapons into the cages, mowing down prisoners behind the iron bars, rats in a barrel. They were tossing something on the bodies. As he passed strewed bodies, he found playing cards, the ace of spades with a grinning death's-head resting on lifeless grimaces.

Muhdal wondered if they were murdering his own men, when, rounding the corner, thrust down the bisecting corridor that led to the north exit, he spotted Zeki and Balik being hustled outside by another squad of invaders manhandling the rest of his fighters for the open door, barking at them in a mix of Kurd and Russian the whole way. Whoever these hooded killers were, they were professionals, he decided, wondering how they had taken down the prison so swiftly, no Turk resistance he could find anywhere. As long as they weren't Americans—who aided and abetted the Ankara regime—he figured he could live with the indignity of a piss shower for the moment, if salvation from Dyrik was guaranteed. Still, he wouldn't forget his shame.

Muhdal kept moving, saw several of the invaders spear bayonets through chests of downed Turks, gutting one or two like pigs, innards gushing to the floor. The vile stench was so strong now bile wormed up his chest, hot slime rolling into his throat. And he spotted the smoke and flames leaping up through the grate in the floor of another wing, two fuel drums dumped on their sides. He picked up his pace, eager to put distance to the screams of men burning alive.

Muhdal hit the courtyard, grateful for fresh air, found the invaders ushering his men into the bellies of three Black Hawk gunships. The guard quarters had been reduced to flaming rubble, he saw, likewise the motor pool of HumVees and troop carriers, nothing but burning scrap. Forging into rotor wash, he gave the grounds and walls a quick search, spotted parachute canopies billowed out by heated wind. A look at the guard towers, he saw bodies draped over railings, the claws of four grappling hooks dug into the top edges of the wall.

Professionals, all right, he thought, aware the attack on the prison had been split down the middle between the invaders. Snipers, creeping in from the steppe, took out the guards, scaled the walls, the other half dropping square into the belly to blast and burn.

Nearing the Black Hawk, the Barking Hood on his heels, urging speed, Muhdal looked to the distant northern sky. There, the sky strobed, blackness peppered to near daylight with brilliant white flashes. He knew there was a large Turk military base in that direction, thought he heard the rumbling of explosions, but the sound was muted by rotor wash.

He boarded the gunship, glanced at Balik before he was shoved to sit. He seethed, staring at the Barking Hood, another invader looking up from the green glow of a laptop monitor. White teeth flashed, a thumbs-up from the other invader, and the Barking Hood laughed.

Suddenly Muhdal felt as if he were quagmired in a nightmare, skin on fire, heart pumping with fury. Who were they? What did they want? They might have known who he was, but they didn't know that, make no mistake, he would return the favor for dousing him in his cell.

The Barking Hood turned, stripped off the com link as the gunship lifted off. As the man tugged off the hood, Muhdal stared up at a face, purpled and cratered around the eyes and jaws from past battle souvenirs, the whole grisly picture as sharp as the edge of a razor, it could have been the skull on the ace of spades.

The big commando chuckled. "Cheer up, Moody. We're here to help make you all rich men."

Muhdal felt his heart lurch, jaw drop. "Americans?"

The Skull laughed. "Yeah, well, they say even the Devil can speak in all tongues."

Speechless, anchored by fear, Muhdal wondered what horror lay in Kurd futures, staring into the Skull's laughing eyes.

"You do believe in the Devil, don't you, Moody? You damn well better—you're looking at him."

HE WAS CALLED Acheron, named for his resurrection after both the river of Greek mythology in Hades, and the demon who guarded the gates of Hell.

It was the sweetest thing, he thought, Judas bastards oblivious he was risen from the dead. Physically speaking, of course, it was impossible to breathe life into oneself, arise from ashes and dust, but the metaphor worked for him; he was alive and doing fine. Thanks to Big Brother, the old Michael Mitchell was long dead and gone, but Acheron was moving on into the night to settle that score, silence an unclean tongue.

And on national television, no less.

Acheron, he thought—he liked that, seeing himself as the living ghost of the charred bones of that skeleton body double from a forgotten covert war zone in Syria. Oh, he was back, all right, feeling good, strong, ready to grab center stage on the Josh Randall show, pull a dagger from the back of the operation of the ages.

With one final look over his shoulder he found the Clairmont Studio lot clear of mortals, then keyed the guest door open. The kid at the gate had been easy, one shot through the forehead with the throwaway sound-suppressed Walther M-6, but he had counted on the bogus *Washington Post* press pass to get him close enough to the booth, eliminate one problem, confiscate keys. That left two armed rental badges inside, he knew, certain his professional talent would drop a couple of overweight play-babies who seemed more inclined to walk female employees to their cars after hours than patrol the premises between doughnuts and coffee. Nailing down the routine of the security detail—so much sloppiness and laziness, he stopped counting the errors of their ways thirty minutes into his first watch—his escape route was mapped out, dry-runned when he wasn't surveying the studio from his high-rise apartment directly across Connecticut Avenue. This, he figured, would prove so easy it was damn near criminal.

Snicking the door closed behind, he found the hall empty, focused on the lights and the chatter of fools at the end of the corridor. Snugging the dark sunglasses tight with a forefinger, his former Company boss wouldn't recognize him, he knew, not until he spoke the bastard's handle. Black wig, mustache and goatee pasted on, it was a shame, he considered, that other traitors may be watching the left wing circle jerk tonight and never know who made the special guest appearance. Well, what was fifteen minutes of fame anyway, when there were years of glory and pleasure at the end of the golden road, beyond his return from the dead?

Marching, he unzipped the loose-fitting windbreaker, pockets weighted down with two exit goodies, twin .50-Magnum Desert Eagles, the showstoppers. It was a bonus, he recalled, cozying up to the makeup girl at the neighborhood pub, plying her with drinks. She couldn't have drawn the setup any better. The stage then, would be off to the right, two cameramen, ten o'clock, rentals on standby, in case an unruly guest needed the hook. It happened, he knew, or so he heard, the punk star so extreme sometimes in left-wing diatribe, even the rational of viewpoint had taken a lunge at his mustache. By God, what he wouldn't give himself, he thought, to rip that mustache off his face, ram it down his gullet...

The coming statement would suffice.

A few paces from the studio, and he heard the loudmouth in question—LIQ—snorting at something the kid said. "With all due respect," LIQ rebuked, "Josh, I was there. Your sources aren't quite on the money. I'm telling you there's a secret paramilitary infrastructure of assassins and saboteurs working for the United States government."

No shit, Acheron thought. And why did the talking dickheads always soften the verbal blow "with all due respect"? Politicians were the worst of flim-flam artists, he thought, all their "quite frankly" and "to be quite honest with you" spelling out they lied the rest of the time. Let that be him up there, he'd tell the punk, "With all due kiss my ass, here's the real deal."

Stow the righteous anger, he told himself. This was business.

The canister, tossed and bouncing up in the heart of the staff, led the entrance, gas spewing a cloud of noxious fumes. Their reaction was typical, expected: cries of panic flayed the air, clipboards and cue cards fell, a mad scramble of bodies ricocheted off one another. He compounded the terror, the Desert Eagle out and pealing. Two heartbeats' worth of thunder blasting through the studio, he tagged the cameramen first, 250-grain boattails exploding through ribs, hurling them back, deadweight bowling down one of the rentals.

The act sticking to the script, he knew he was still live and in color, coast to coast. He was a star right then, and shine he would.

Another tap of the trigger, and he glimpsed a bright red cloud erupt out the back of the standing rental, bodies thrashing and hacking their way out of the tear gas. Tracking on, he dropped Rental Number Three as he staggered to his feet, a head shot, leaving no doubt. With only seconds to wrap it up, exit stage left, Acheron swung his aim stageward. The kid bleated out what sounded like a plea, the star shrill next in demand his life be spared, silk-suited arms flapping. Acheron blew him out of his seat.

Rolling toward the raised platform, Acheron found the

ZIQ glued to his chair, hands raised. What the hell? Obviously the guy had gone soft, a civilian life of fame and small fortune dulling the edge of former killer instincts and battlefield reflex. Where he remembered the ZIQ once lean and hard, Acheron saw a double decker chin, coiffed hair, pink manicured fingers, a goddamn walrus in Armani, he thought.

The former CIA assassin drew a bead between wide eyes, flipped the calling card on the table.

Fat quivered under the man's jowl as he looked up from the ace of spades with a death's-head. "You?"

"With all due kiss my ass—you're a dirty rat bastard, Captain Jack."

"Wait!"

"Waited more than ten years already," Acheron said, and squeezed the trigger.

FRAMED IN SOFT LIGHT, they stared back, a living malevolence, it felt, mocking sleepless nights, telling him they would come for a day of reckoning.

"The rebel angels have risen from the pit."

How could it be possible? he wondered. Another shot of whiskey, and the courage he chased kept running away, an evanescent ray of light in the shadows of his living room.

Over ten years had passed since he and several colleagues hatched the dread warning phrase they hoped none of them would ever need to pass on. Already one of them was dead, the national audience bearing witness to murder, and live on television, for God's sake.

It was happening.

Still, Timothy Balton wanted to believe it was some grotesque prank by former colleagues, perhaps envious of his early retirement, that he carved himself a slice of peace and quiet, or maybe angry he turned away from them after a life of service and dedication to national security. Unfortunately there was this blight—off the record—on his career, haunting them all for more than a decade.

Their deaths had been confirmed—sort of. After those two covert debacles, which never came to the attention of any Senate committee on intelligence or counterterrorism, even the President of the United States kept in the dark, the rumor mill churned, casting specters of grave doubt and fear over the headshed in the loop. The best forensics teams the NSA and the CIA could marshal stated, off the record, they couldn't be one-hundred-percent certain the burned remains were those of Alpha Deep Six. Then there were the slush funds for black ops in secret numbered accounts, twenty million and change whisked into cyberspace following their supposed demise. Well, the horrible truth behind the vanishing act leaked out when the headshed's cover-up was launched in dark earnest. A few crumbs of intel, however, tossed their way, here and there, by followers deemed nonessential personnel and cheated by Alpha Deep Six of their own payday only magnified the enormity of the agenda. As former head of the DOD's Classified Military Aircraft-Classified Military Flights—CMA-CMF—he discovered, during a yearlong follow-up investigation, low and high tech jets, cargo planes and helicopters were vanishing from CIA, DIA and NSA bases and installations from Nevada to Afghanistan. The bodies of personnel responsible for guarding such aircraft began stacking up so fast, no witnesses, no clues, not a shred of evidence as to the identities of the assassins left behind, it struck him as if...

What? That all of them had been executed by murderous phantoms?

Trembling, he poured another dose from the half-empty bottle. Down the hatch, hands steady moments later, enough so he felt confident he could aim and fire the Taurus PT-58 with deadly accuracy. He pulled the CD-ROM from the desk drawer. Say they did come? What then? Hand Alpha Deep Six the gathered intelligence on all secrets known about them?

Give up the details, hoping they would spare his life, about their disappearance and purported resurrection, what they had allegedly initiated as part of an agenda so horrific he now considered it the evil of the ages?

Evil, he knew, that he was, albeit indirectly, responsible for loosing on the world.

He stared at the picture on his desk. Choking back tears, he wondered if he would soon join his wife and only son.

He flinched, wind howling outside, pistol up as he pivoted toward the curtained windows, something banging off the wall. Shadows, it looked, danced in the night world. Could be, he thought, just moonlight, shining through scudding clouds. Wind, he knew, often gusted over the plain, stirred south from the Badlands.

He hesitated, then laid down the weapon. One more shot, he told himself, he desperately needed sleep, if only for an hour. He was thinking he should check the alarm system one more time, recon the ranch and perimeter when—

"So, I understand you want divine knowledge."

Balton froze. He felt them, no need to turn, he discovered, three shadows flickering over the wall. His hand shook as he reached for the pistol. He felt a strange urge to laugh, amazed and terrified how easily they breached his security net, but knew they had the technology, able to burn out the guts of a warning system, laser beams melting alarms and motion sensors to molten goo, no matter how complex. It was over, he knew; it was simply a question of how it would end, how soon, how much pain he would endure.

"Cramnon," he breathed.

"Richard Cramnon's dead, remember? I am Abbadon."

"What?"

"I have been raised up from the dead as Abbadon. That would be ancient Hebrew for 'destruction.' I am the bottomless pit, consuming the damned in eternal fire. I am the abyss that vomits forth the dark angel to spread plague and death across the earth."

"You're insane."

"No. I have never been more right."

Balton felt his heart skip a beat, a rumble of cold laughter striking his back.

"Don't look so puked out, Timothy. We just came by to say we love you." His laughter echoed by the others, Cramnon went on, "By the way, I was real sorry to hear about your wife. Breast cancer, huh. Pity about your boy, too. Heroin, was it?" He laughed.

"You rotten son of a—"

"Drugs, modern-day scourge, I always said, the invisible foreign invasion. Hey, they say it's a real heartbreaker, a father having to bury his own child. What do you think it was that pushed the little punk over the edge? Kid couldn't live up to your high standards?"

Balton squeezed his eyes shut, heard Cramnon laugh beyond the roaring in his ears.

"Too much pressure from the old man, not enough love and affection? Big shot that you were at DOD, too caught up in work, family always on the backburner. Bet you hated and blamed yourself when you stared into his coffin, huh? Wonder still how such a tragedy could happen? Wish to God you could have it back to do over. Thing about that, Timothy, human beings always wish they could do it over, make it right, the old 'if I knew then what I know now.' Being a little more than human these days, well, I had a long chat with God while I was away. He told me, among other things, human beings would commit the same damn mistakes even if they could turn back time. Oh, yeah, I was thinking about you, asked God why even bother to create your son if the punk was going to cause you such grief. God, He tells me humans are always crying, 'why?' when they should ask 'how?' As in how to fix, how to find a solution. That's why I'm here…the disk?"

Shaking, Balton began to turn, aiming his rage toward their laughter. He hoped his body concealed the Taurus, long enough where he could at least tag one, two if he got lucky. He was in slow motion, dizzied by shock, as if he faced the three of them. The one he believed was Cramnon appeared to float across the room, a tall shadow in long black coat, rolling counterclockwise from the other two shadows peeling the other way. Pistol coming around, trigger taking up slack, he balked, shocked how different they looked than he remembered. Where they were once clean cut and fair skinned, he found hair, as black as a raven, flowing to their shoulders. With prominent cheekbones and hawk noses, complexions so dark or burnished by sun, black eyes that were once blue they appeared...

Semitic?

A shot cracked from the dark. He heard a sharp grunt, pistol flying from his hand, then froze at the sight of blood jetting from the stump where his thumb was amputated. Balton slumped, clutched his hand, gagged.

"Your boy Gulliver, I made it last two days before he gave you up."

Balton heard his bitter chuckle, then felt tears welling as he looked at the picture. So this was how it would end, he thought, the world fading, the blood pumping out. So many mistakes, so much neglect dead-ending in too much pain and sorrow. It galled him, but Cramnon's cruel words rang true, ground deep. They—whoever they were, he thought—said a man's character was his destiny. Strange, he decided, he wasn't sure what was his own true character. Way beyond guilt and regret now—again, "they" claimed not even God could change the past, and, yes, that even the Devil knew the darkest corners of human hearts, the worst pain, the most atrocious of every man's thoughts and desires—he suddenly prayed to a divine being he hadn't thought about since his wife died. He heard the evil thing demand the disk. Brushing it to the edge of the desk, he heard, "And the password?"

Why not? "Agrippa."

He shut out the laughter, silently implored for a quick, merciful end he knew he didn't deserve. He prayed for forgiveness, his own sins too many, he thought, to even recall. He glimpsed one of the shadows falling beside him, slip the disk into the computer. A metallic click behind, smoke blew over his head, Cramnon laughing about the irony of the password. Something about how Agrippa was an ancient sorcerer's book, pages made of human skin, how it listed the names of every demon in Hell, how they could be summoned to earth to help the caller fulfill whatever desire and wish.

"We're in business," Balton heard the shadow say.

Then Cramnon asked, "You prefer it in the back?"

He straightened, offered up a last silent prayer this monstrous evil was soon, somehow, removed from the face of the earth, sent where it belonged, before it was too late.

Turning, he told Cramnon, "No."

1

If the nation's enemies pulled it off, Mack Bolan feared the United States of America would cease to exist as he knew it. Any number of apocalyptic nightmares charged through his mind, stoked a sense of dire urgency while inflaming a righteous anger he hadn't felt in some time. Martial law, he knew, would prove the least of the nation's woes. The shortlist of horrors spewed from the brewing cauldron of this hell—looting, riots, interstates and highways parking lots as panicked civilians fled for the hills, murder in the streets by those left behind in the chaos and terror—was incomprehensible to rational human minds.

Unfortunately, he had walked this road many times in his War Everlasting. And he knew all about the cannibals unleashing death and destruction on free and not so free societies, consuming or oppressing the innocent, driven by whatever dark machinations churned in hearts pumping with the blood of the wicked.

Only this crisis defied any past experience Bolan had ever known.

Wedged in the doorway beside the M-60 gunner, the Black Hawk gunship sailing over the wooded countryside of Williamsburg, Bolan took in the command-and-control center. A quick head count, as the warbird descended, and he figured ten to fifteen special ops ringing the farmhouse perimeter. Four Black Hawks were grounded in the distance, fuel bladders, he found, already dropped off for quick topping out of tanks, one critical detail out of the way.

Slashed by midmorning sunshine, there were too many black sedans to bother counting—government-issue vehicles having delivered the best and brightest from the FBI, NSA, DIA and whoever else muscled their way into the game—he then noted the small armada of oversize vans in matching color. High-tech communications-surveillance-tracking centers on wheels, bristling with antennae, spouting sat dishes, they could garner intelligence at light speed. From past hands-on experience with war wagons, he knew they could mobilize and steer field operatives to the enemy's back door before they were aware the sky was falling.

Panning on, he saw satellite dishes, staggered at various intervals, fanning away from the C-and-C center, cables hooked into generators mounted in the beds of Army transport trucks or HumVees. It appeared top-notch professional on the surface, but it was an operation marshaled in a few short hours, he knew, backed with the full blessing of an anxious White House and Pentagon. And the political-military powers had damn good reason to feel the collective knot in their belly. Sometimes, though, haste, edging toward panic in this case, he thought, led to bad decisions. Warning bells told him there were too many chiefs in the act.

There was some good news, a ray of hope they could abort the enemy's twisted dream. The FBI had grabbed four of them—two in Richmond, two in Fredericksburg—Bolan learned during his initial briefing at the Justice Department. Under interrogation, the Feds had a general idea what was unfolding, but no clear fix on enemy numbers, where and when the big event—as the opposition called it—would happen. With their arrest, a nervous logic rippled down the chain of intelligence and military command, the former capital of Virginia chosen for strategic purposes, central command planted between what were believed intended strike points. Virginia Beach south, Richmond and Washington, D.C., due north, and Baltimore a short hop up the interstate from there, if the opposition was already on the move, if the enemy even partly succeeded...

Intelligence at this point, he knew, had to be on the money if he was to root out, crush the scourge before it unleashed its murderous agenda.

And hunting down the savages was the reason why he was there.

The Black Hawk touching down, Bolan bounded out the doorway, forged into rotor wash. Closing on the front porch, he found beefed-up security nearly invisible to the naked eye. Briefly he wondered how his sudden entrance into the hunt would be received, an unknown marching in with carte blanche to call the shots. On that score, all egos needed to take a back seat, he knew, as he glimpsed blacksuited men hunkered in the woods, Stoner 63 Light Machine Guns poking through brush, figures with FBI stenciled on wind-breakers, Armalite AR-18 assault rifles slung around their shoulders, Feds scurrying in and out of the intel nerve center.

His orders were clear. And a presidential directive had cut through red tape, dropped him square in charge. If anybody had problems with that, there was a number to call, a direct line to the President. The Man in the Oval Office, and Hal Brognola, the big Fed at the Justice Department who gave him his marching orders, knew the credentials he was bringing here were bogus, but they were likewise aware this was no time for interagency backbiting and grandstanding.

It was the eleventh hour, time for decisive, swift and, hopefully, preemptive action.

Or else...

The grim thought trailed away as he saw the tall FBI man materialize in the doorway, venture a few steps across the porch, then appear to balk at what he saw.

"You Special Agent Matt Cooper?"

Of course, the FBI man knew that already, the coded message radioed ahead before his Black Hawk breached their airspace. "That would be me."

"Agent Michael James. ASAC, now that you're here."

"What do you have?"

"What we've got are definite major 'effing' problems."

"How about telling me something I don't know?"

He pulled up short, watching as ASAC James looked him up and down, the FBI man perhaps wondering more "what" he was than "who." No question, he looked military, specifically black ops, worlds apart from any G-man, he knew. Start with the dark aviator shades, for instance, then the combat blacksuit, his tried and proved lethal duo of side arms filling out the windbreaker. There was the Beretta 93-R in shoulder holster, the mammoth .44 Magnum Desert Eagle riding his hip, for killing starters. Just above the rubber-soled combat boots, a Ka-bar fighting knife was sheathed around his shin, just in case all else failed. Combat vest, pouches slitted to house spare clips, webbing lined with a bevy of frag, tear gas, flash-stun and incendiary grenades, and whatever else he needed for battle, urban or otherwise, was bagged in nylon in the gunship.

"Come on, we're on the clock, Cooper."

Inside the nerve center, trailing James, Bolan felt the air of controlled frenzy, a hornet's nest of buzzing activity. Banks of computers, digital monitors and wall maps packing the room with inches to spare, he navigated through the web of cables strung across the floor. Above the electronic chitter and voices relaying intelligence over com links and secured sat phones, he heard James say, "We think there may be as many as six to ten cells, according to electronic intercepts, surveillance, what cooperation we've gotten from their own communities, informants, here and abroad, on our payroll, filling in a few particulars. In the plus column, we grabbed another of these assholes in Boston. He appears willing to talk, but I'm hearing he's second or third tier, meaning he was on need-to-know until the last minute before the big bang. We don't know if the cells are working in twos, threes or as independent operators, nor what their specific destinations of target."

James stopped by a bank of monitors tied into fax machines, sat phones. "Another sliver of sunlight—two more were snatched at Penn Station, while you were in the air. They were minutes from boarding the Number 90 and 93 trains. Two carry-ons per scumbag, four bags, all loaded with Semtex, the payload just inside Amtrak's fifty-pound limit. Military explosive. Begs the question how the hell they got their hands on it, where and from who in the first place. First-class tickets, one way, of course, they were booked two cars down from the river's seat. That much wallop, we figure at least two cars trashed and gone up in flames, complete derailment, the works rolling up, one car after…"

"I've got the picture."

"Okay. We are on ThreatCon Delta, terrorist alert severe. If you could ratchet it up a notch the country would be under martial law. You can well imagine the panic already out there among John and Jane Q. Citizen, what with the media jamming mikes and cameras in the face of anybody who looks official. All local and state law enforcement have been scrambled to aid and assist the National Guard, the Army, Special Forces, Delta in the shutdowns, searches, sealing off perimeters of all terminals and depots, starting with the major cities, particularly the Eastern Seaboard, the West Coast. If we don't chop them off at the knees, and soon, well—"

"Airports?"

"Security personnel and procedures have been quadrupled, but we're reading this as a whole different ballgame than using jumbo jets as flying bombs. Just the same, the skies are swarming with every fighter jet we can put in the air. Incoming international air traffic, especially executive jets, will be intercepted and escorted to landing. No compliance, bye-bye, that's straight from the White House. Same thing with ships, large, small, pleasure or commercial. The Coast Guard and the Navy have formed a steel wall, up and down both shore-lines, likewise the Gulf."

Was it enough? Bolan wondered. It was a task so monu-mental it boggled the mind. No amount of manpower, no matter how skilled or determined, could one-hundred-per-cent guarantee a few of the opposition didn't slip through the net. Then there were trains, buses already rolling, loaded with unsuspecting passengers, potential conflagrations on wheels that could detonate any moment. He looked at the monitors, saw numbers scrolling as fast as personnel could scoop up sheafs of printed paper. Digital maps of Chicago, New York, Seattle, Los Angeles, Miami were yielding the locations of train and bus terminals, points of travel, layovers and final des-tinations, all flashing up in red.

"So far, we've sealed off and stopped all departures from Seattle's King Street Station. We're working on Union Sta-tion in D.C. now," James said. "You have Metrorail, the VRE, MARC, and that's just Washington to worry about. The list is near endless as far as manpower is concerned, covering all bases. We're stopping trains and buses that are in transit—as we can get to them—board, clear them out, search all luggage, but it's going to take time, something we don't have. We've just alerted the Chicago Transit Authority. They are under presidential directive to shut down Union Station on Canal Street, but as you might know, Chicago is considered the rail-way center of the country. God only knows how many trains we're looking at, arriving or leaving in or within a hundred miles around the compass of Chicago alone. You're talking over two hundred trains, rolling anywhere along some twenty-four thousand miles of track at any given time. I don't even have the numbers crunched yet on how many Greyhound, Trailways and charter and tour-bus terminals and depots we have that may be in their crosshairs. There's more," he said, paused. "The headsheds are thinking there could even be eighteen-wheelers, vans, U-Haul trucks out there, cab and limo drivers…you get the picture? If this thing blows up in our faces, the entire transportation network of the United States is shut down, end of story. Even if they set off one, two trains or buses, and you've got wreckage and dead bodies all over the highways and tracks, I don't even want to hazard a guess as to the chaos that would break out."

"I want everything you have in ten minutes."

"You've got it?"

"I'm thinking we might be able to narrow our problems down in short order."

"How so?" James asked.

"Where are the prisoners?"

James grunted, jerked a nod to the deep corner of the room where an armed guard stood. "In the cellar. Problem is, we've already lost two of the four."

"What are you talking about?"

"I'm afraid the show's already started without you. I have to warn you, Cooper, it's messy down there. His name is Moctaw, or that's what he calls himself."

"What is he?"

"I don't know, but he was dumped in my lap, damn near a suitcase load of official DOD papers telling me I was to step aside—that is if I wanted to finish my career with the FBI. There was nothing I could do."

A sordid picture of what he was about to find downstairs already in mind, Bolan followed James across the room, the FBI man barking for the guard to step aside and open the door.

"I'll leave you to introduce yourself," James said, wheeled, then marched back for the nerve center.

Peering into the gloomy shadows below, he caught a whiff of the miasma, an invisible blow to his senses. It was a sickening mix of blood cooked flesh, loosed body waste. He heard the sharp grunts, then a scream echoed up from the pit.

He slipped off his shades, braced for the horror he knew was down there, waiting.

Then Mack Bolan, also known as the Executioner, began his descent.

HER NAME WAS Barbara Price, and it was rare when she left her post at Stony Man Farm. She was, after all, mission controller for the Justice Department's ultracovert Sensitive Operations Group, her time and expertise on demand nearly around the clock. It was both her present role in covert operations at the Farm, however, and her past employment at the National Security Agency that now found her moments away from rendezvousing with a former colleague.

She watched the numbers on the doors fall, striding down the hallway, looked at a couple pass her by through sunglasses, her low-heeled slip-ons padding over wall-to-wall carpet. She couldn't shake the feeling something felt wrong about this setup. She hadn't survived, nor claimed her current position with the Sensitive Operations Group, by taking anything in the spook world at face value.

Since being informed by cutouts she often used to gather intelligence that Max Geller sounded desperate in his attempts to reach her, a dark nagging had hounded her for days. She hadn't seen, heard from or thought about the man in years, and there he was, hunting her down for undeclared reasons, popping up on the radar screen, out of nowhere.

Finally she returned his call through a series of back channels she arranged. It was the worst of times to leave the Farm, Able Team and Phoenix Force in the trenches, with Mack Bolan, the Farm's lone-wolf operative and a man she was, on occasion, intimate with, in the field. But Geller claimed to have critical information about what the Stony Man warriors were up against, likewise alluding to a threat so grave to national security the entire world could be changed forever. No, he didn't dare speak on any line, no matter how secure. They had to meet.

She had run it past Hal Brognola, the big Fed at the Justice Department who was director of the Farm and liaison to the President. He had given her three hours' leave, but she was to call the time and place for the meet, give him the particulars before she set out. The chopper had ferried her from the Shenandoah Valley to Reagan National, where the Justice Department maintained a small hangar, kept its own vehicles on-site for quick personal access, instead of using "invented" credit cards for rentals. From there in the GMC, a short drive to the hotel in Crystal City, where the feeling she was being followed intensified. It was nothing she could put her finger on, though. Crystal City swarm with the work force that early-morning hour, a lone blond woman sure to grab the attention of men. Taking extra precautions, just the same, she sat in the hotel lot for fifteen minutes, her instincts flaring so bad she almost called off the meet. A short drive around Crystal City, then she parked in an underground garage, wondered if she was being paranoid. Follow through, she decided. She'd come this far, maybe Geller had something worth hearing. She was grateful, just the same, that the Browning Hi-Power with 13-shot clip was shouldered beneath the windbreaker, two backup clips leathered on her right side.

She found the door to the room where he'd registered under James Wilcox. It had been years since she had worked with the man, both of them gathering signals intelligence and human intelligence for the NSA in a classified program that often involved her directing wet work. Geller was the best at what he did. Tagged the Sphinx, he still was, she knew, the NSA's best code breaker.

She knocked, waited, glanced both ways down the empty hall, removed her sunglasses. The door opened so quickly that she wondered if he had X-ray eyes or had been standing on the foyer, waiting, listening.

"Thanks for coming."

The whiskey fumes swarmed her senses, the first red flag

warning her again this felt all wrong. He wasn't the slim, sharply-dressed, well-groomed man she remembered. He had aged terribly, gained weight, lost hair. But it was the eyes, sunken with dark circles, unable to focus on her, brimmed with so much anxiety she could smell the fear in the sweat soaked into the collar of his sports shirt. She almost turned, walked away, but he beckoned her to enter.

She did.

"AND JUST WHO the fuck might you be?"

Bolan looked at the ghoul, said, "I was just about to ask you the same thing."

The soldier found it was every bit as messy down there as James warned, and then some. Bolan felt a ball of cold anger lodge in his belly at what he saw in the bastard's torture chamber. It was gruesome devil's work to the extreme, and he couldn't even begin to tally how many laws the butcher had broken. He was fairly certain, though, whichever agency the man pledged allegiance to had given him the green light to do whatever it took to break the prisoners, that he was backed and covered by superiors who would, most likely, wash their hands of this horror show. Yes, Bolan knew the argument— extreme times demanding extreme measures and so forth— but torture in his mind only reduced a man to the same soulless animal level as the enemy. It sickened him to know Moctaw worked for the same government he did. Then again, it occurred to him Moctaw had bulled ahead, aware someone else was on the way to take the reins, the butcher running some personal agenda. Gain information, or threaten the prisoners about talking to the Feds? Every instinct Bolan had earned over the years—fighting every ilk of backstabbing home-grown traitor—warned him something didn't jibe with the man or his methods. Something else lurked behind the mask, he was sure. Any front Moctaw would put on that was all done in the name of national security was a ruse. Whom was he protecting? What was he hiding? Or was this simply an extreme solution to the dilemma of fighting terrorism on American soil?

Bolan looked at the prisoners. Naked, they were strapped to thick wooden chairs, which were bolted to the concrete floor. There were two bodies, a dark hole between their eyes. The soldier figured they were the lucky ones. The other two prisoners had some sort of steel vise holding their heads erect, clamps fastened to their eyebrows, their eyes bulging with terror, flicking around like pinballs at their tormentor. Whoever this Moctaw was, Bolan saw he was good with the Gestapo tactics. The black bag, opened on the table, had been emptied of a series of shiny surgical instruments, one of which was a bloody pair of shears. Torniquets, Bolan saw, were wound around the wrists and ankles of the dead men, all of their fingers and toes strewed in the blood still pooling on the floor. At some point, the bastard had castrated his first two victims, genitals adding to the gory mess at the stumps of their feet. It was obvious where the cigar in the butcher's hand would have gone next. One glance at Moctaw, and Bolan pegged him as little more than a thug. Six-six at least, the muscled Goliath swelled out the black leather apron, blood speckling his craggy features, red drops still falling from a dark mane of disheveled hair. In the tight confines of mildewed brick the stench alone was damn near enough to make even a battle-hardened soldier like Bolan gag. Then he saw the series of oozing burn holes running up the torsos, necks, cheeks, the bastard working his way up, letting them know they were seconds away from having their eyes seared out.

Bolan produced his credentials, thrust them in Moctaw's face. The butcher grunted, unimpressed, or disappointed, the soldier couldn't tell. "Your fun's over."

"Special Agent Matt Cooper, uh-huh. I heard about you."

"Then you heard I'm in charge. That's straight from the White House. You're out of it."

"Out of it? This one here," he snarled, shoving the glowing end of the cigar toward the prisoner at the far end, "was just about to talk."

"I'll handle it from here."

"You'll handle it? What—you going to bring them some cookies and milk? Sweet-talk 'em? Maybe offer them some all-expenses-paid deal if they sing?"

Bolan stepped around the table, saw the Beretta 92-F within easy reach of the butcher. "Give me the cigar."

It was a dangerous moment, Bolan watching as Moctaw wrestled with some decision, the soldier braced for the butcher to make a grab for the weapon. Moctaw bared his teeth, dumped the cigar on the table.

"It's your party, G-boy. I hope you're not just some six-pack of asskick, all show, no go, since you're the man of the hour now. Maybe you don't know it, but this country's entire transportation system is on the verge of being shut down, I'm talking 9/11 five, maybe ten times over, depending on how many of these scumbags are out there. This is no time for 'pretty please.'"

Bolan made his own decision right then, picked up the cigar. "I'm aware of what's at stake."

"Really? These Red Crescent terrorists pull off their big event, shit, we're going to need Iraqi oil revenue ourselves to help put it all back together. This country will never be the same, they light up even one train or a couple of Greyhounds."

"Besides your gift for stating the obvious, exactly what have you learned?"

Moctaw hesitated, then picked up one of four small square black boxes from the table. The clips-on gave Bolan a good idea of what they were, then Moctaw confirmed it, saying, "These are satellite-relay pagers. Far as we know, only the Russians and the Israelis, and maybe the Chinese and North Koreans, have this sort of technology."

"And the NSA and the CIA."

Moctaw hesitated. "Right. There are no markings, no serial numbers on these. I couldn't tell you where they came from. They house computer chips that can tie into military communications satellites. Punch in your personal code, hooks you into the principal user, you can beep or be beeped, send or be sent a vibrating signal anywhere from three to five thousand miles. That's how they knew to move."

"Which means whoever's running the operation is still out there."

"That would be a good assumption. We've learned they were communicating by courier when they set up shop, or used P.O. boxes. Basic keep it simple. For the most part they stayed off the phone, e-mail, Internet, but a couple of them got antsy, even made some overseas calls back home to their loved ones to say goodbye and they were on their way to Paradise. Not real smart. We were able to intercept—"

"I know all that."

Moctaw scowled, then continued, "The usual bogus passports, only they come to America as Europeans, dyed hair, clean shaved, perfect English. Never know they were camel jockeys. Two of them," he said, nodding at the corpses, "were Iraqis, former fedayeen, to be exact. Made a point of letting me know they were going to blow up some buses and trains, jihad for Gulf II, standard Muslim-fanatic tirade. The two still breathing are Moroccan, recruited, they tell me, in Casablanca by Red Crescent about a year ago." Moctaw pulled the Greyhound tickets from his bag, slapped them on the table. "Four one-way tickets. Two heading north, Port Authority. The other two were westbound, final stop Houston. I've got their ordnance upstairs. Three hundred pounds of Semtex between them, wired and ready to be activated by radio remote."

Bolan looked at the tickets. "Richmond," he said, noting the gate numbers and times of departure. Checking his watch, he found they were due to leave in an hour, give or take. It stood to reason they had been en route to link up with another cell, in Richmond or beyond. He stuffed the tickets in a pocket.

"You have a plan, or are you here to profile, Cooper?"

"What are their names?" Bolan asked, produced a lighter, then put the flame to the end of the cigar.

"I was calling them Ali Baba, one through four."

Bolan puffed on the cigar until the tip glowed. "I could have you arrested."

"Not if you're about to do what I think you are."

"I still might cuff and stuff you."

"You could try."

"Telling me whoever you work for has clout."

"This thing isn't being run by the White House. You could have the President arrest me himself, and I'd be out and free in less than an hour. And, no, I won't tell you who I work for. You do your own homework."

Bolan blew smoke in Moctaw's face. There was no time for the hassle of arresting the man, get mired in a pissing contest. Besides, the more he heard from Moctaw the more the bells and whistles rang and blew louder. If he let the man remain at large, he decided, he might end up using him to chum the waters.

Bolan turned his attention to the prisoners. Sometimes, he knew, the threat of torture, especially if a man faced permanent mutilation, worked better than the act itself. One look at the terror bugging out the eyes, bodies quaking, limbs straining to break their bounds, and he knew Moctaw had brought them to the breaking point. They just needed another shove.

The Executioner showed them the glowing tip, then puffed, working the eye to cherry red, let the smoke drift over their faces, choking them. "What are your names?"

"Khariq…"

"Mah…moud…"

"You have two choices," Bolan said. "Tell me everything you know about your end of the operation. If you do that, and we find you're just foot soldiers, no previous track record of terrorism, no blood on your hands, there's a chance you eventually will be sent home to your families. I have the power to be able to make your freedom happen."

"Cooper, you do not have—"

"Shut up," the Executioner growled over his shoulder. He put menace in his eyes and voice that would have even made Moctaw flinch, he believed, leaning closer to their faces, holding the end of the cigar inches from a bulging orb. He saw tears break from the eye as it felt the heat. "One eye at a time." He flicked his lighter, waved the flame around. "While I work on your eyes, I'll put this to your balls. This is not good cop-bad cop."

"We talk…we talk…."

And they did. Bolan stepped back, listening as they babbled so fast he had to slow them down, one at a time. They were to meet three more Red Crescent operatives in Richmond. Bolan got a description of both their attire and the duffel bags with custom designs. Two would be attached to each half of the four-man cell, then they would split off at other depots along the way. The lone operative out was the question mark; they didn't know what his role was. Bolan figured the odd terrorist out for the cell leader. Then the clincher. Enough explosives were going to be left behind in lockers it would be enough to bring down the building.

The Executioner had a critical call to make, but decided to do it in the air while choppering to Richmond. He ground the cigar out on the table. "I'll have James take these prisoners off your hands. He'll take their passports and secure the ordnance."

"That's it? I'm dismissed?"

"No. For your sake you better hope I never lay eyes on you again."

Moctaw made some spitting noise, an expression hardening his face Bolan read as "We'll see." The Executioner put the ghoul out of mind, bounding up the steps. The doomsday clock, he feared, was ticking down to maybe a handful of minutes.

James Axler
Outlanders®

EVIL ABYSS

An ancient kingdom harbors awesome secrets...

In the heart of Cambodia, a portal to the eternal mysteries of space and time lures both good and evil to its promise. Now, a deadly imbalance has not only brought havoc to the region, but it also threatens the efforts of the Cerberus warriors. To have control of the secrets locked deep within the sacred city is to possess the power to manipulate earth's vast energies...and in the wrong hands, to alter the past, present and future in unfathomable ways....

Available February 2005 at your favorite retail outlet.

TAKE 'EM FREE
2 action-packed novels plus a mystery bonus
NO RISK
NO OBLIGATION TO BUY

DEATH LANDS®

Shaking Earth

*Available December 2004
at your favorite retail outlet.*

In a land steeped in ancient legend, power and destruction, the crumbling ruins of what was once Mexico City are now under siege by a bloodthirsty tribe of aboriginal muties. Emerging from a gateway into the partially submerged ruins of this once great city, Ryan and his group ally themselves with a fair and just baron caught in a treacherous power struggle with a dangerous rival. An internecine war foreshadows ultimate destruction of the valley at a time when unity of command and purpose offers the only hope against a terrible fate....